Twisted Heartstrings

TWISTED TRAGIC #1

A. KELLY SWEENEY

Dedication

To my family, who have suffered through hours of me being tied to my computer while making my dreams come true. Without your support I would never have taken the chance to make this happen.

Prologue
LUCIUS

Our summer is booked with back-to-back gigs every weekend. Sure, it's only playing in bars, but you have to start somewhere. Yeah, we're stuck doing covers at the moment while we finish working on our first album--we still have a few more songs to finish writing. Our goal is to make enough money this summer to buy some studio time so we can record an album and get our own work out there. We have some amazing songs written already; songs we've spent the last few years working on. It's been a huge learning curve taking what we hear in our heads and transferring it to paper. But we're rising to the challenge, and I'm sure we'll just get better with time.

Tonight we have a show that we're excited about. We have a few gigs lined up for us at the venue over the course of the next few weeks. This venue is one that a lot of people frequent, so we will be getting a lot more exposure than we have at the bars where we've been playing. I can only hope that the girl I've been watching all summer is here; she's been to every show we have played so far.

The DJ is playing music while we start setting our things up. We're early and just want to make sure things are ready for when we go on. Being early also means we can have a drink or two beforehand. One thing we're all aware of is the perks of performing. It wouldn't be hard to pick up chicks. But then again, I'm not looking to score. I just got out of a relationship. We were semi-serious, but she wanted more than what I did at the time. She wanted a bigger commitment. I'm twenty-one, I'm not ready for that right now, and a woman deserves to have someone who can commit to her.

As we play, I can't help but notice my mystery girl in the crowd and I smile to myself, glad that she showed up. She's absolutely gorgeous. I've never been attracted to blondes before, but I find myself attracted to her. The way she moves her body only shows off her figure more. The jeans and tank top she has on form to her body, but I prefer the summer dresses and skirts she's worn in the past. I've been attracted to other girls before, of course, but there's something about her that is different, and I can't figure it out. All summer I've been plagued by wanting to talk to her, but haven't worked up the courage to do it.

When we finish our first set, we head over to the bar to get a drink. I can't help that I keep searching her out in the crowd.

"Luc, you looking for that chick?" Alucard, my brother, asks.

"Yeah," I answer, when my gaze finally finds her.

"Then go talk to her and quit being a pussy. It looks like you might have some competition with the guys buzzing around her and her friend."

I order my drink, hoping to work up the courage to talk to her tonight. I'm not normally the shy one of the group, but for some reason

I haven't figured out how to approach her. The guys have spent the summer trying to get me to talk to her, and it's amused them that I haven't. Al has offered to talk to her for me, but I don't want him near her. I want her for myself. I almost fear that if he talks to her first, she'll want him rather than me.

When we take the stage for our next set I look around for her and smirk when I find her on the dance floor again with her friend. As we play, I let myself get lost in the music, figuring I'll talk to her when the set is done. As always when she's near, I can feel her eyes on me and I can't help but smile. I need to talk to her, soon.

As we load the last of our equipment into the utility trailer that Nic's parents got for us, we can't help but feel excited. Tonight the bar is packed and everyone's having a good time. The guys are wanting to get back in to drink, and I'd like another drink to try to work up the courage to talk to the mystery girl who's been on my mind the whole summer.

Walking toward the bar to order another beer, I can't help but search the crowd for her. I grab the beer my brother has waiting for me and scan the faces again; I don't see her. I feel a little disappointed, she's never left the bar early any time I've seen her.

We enjoy a couple more drinks. Jasper, being our resident DD, will drive us and the gear home. Jasper doesn't drink much, which is how he ends up being our sober driver all the time. He's ok with it, and he doesn't really talk much about why he doesn't drink often. Don't get me wrong, he does enjoy the occasional drink with us, but he doesn't drink a lot.

One week later

We have another gig tonight. We took last night off, mostly because our parents wanted to do their annual end of summer get together. It has become a tradition. At the beginning of the summer we have one to welcome my older brothers home from school, and another at the end of the summer to send them off again. It's a tradition we've kept up even after they finished school. Our dad wasn't pleased that Alucard and I chose not to go to college or university, but our mom supported our choice to go after our dream.

Tonight, I didn't give a shit. Tonight was

going to be the night I finally talked to her. As my brother said, I need to stop being a pussy and just do it. What's the worst she could do? Walk away from me? I doubt it, not after watching her check me and my brother out all summer. I just hoped it was me who she was interested in and not him.

If there's one thing I hate, it's coming in second to my twin brother. For years, Al was always the first to do things. Marius, my oldest brother, was always there to help me get caught up to Al. But when I found out I was better academically than my brother, I was happy. I had finally found something I was better at than him. Then I found the guitar and I was hooked. Al picked up on it too, but I've always been the better of the two and he knew it. It's why when we formed Twisted Tragic, it was decided I'd be lead guitarist and he'd be rhythm. I'll admit that he can be an asshole at times, but he'd freely admit that I'm a better player than he is.

After tonight, we're finally hitting a recording studio in Calgary to start working on our album, so we're a little stoked about that. That's part of what is spurring me on to talk to her; I want to know if I can see her again when I get back from recording.

After we set up for the gig and enjoy a pre-show beer, I keep an eye out for her. My plan is to speak with her while we're on a break between sets. But as we progress into the first set, I'm slightly disappointed that I don't see her. Even during our set break and into the next set I didn't see her. I'm left wondering if I missed my opportunity of getting to know her; if maybe I only had a short window of opportunity. It made me start to question things, like if all things had a shelf life before your chances are gone. Maybe next time I see something I want, I should grab the opportunity while I have the chance.

Chapter One
TONI

Keri and I are pumped with the music flowing around us. She had scored us tickets to see Twisted Tragic. They are one of the hottest up-and-coming rock bands. Their first album was self-published and had gotten them a contract with a major label. Keri and I first heard them years ago in a bar we had frequented when they played covers, and I was so excited to see their success. I knew they had talent and had hoped they would make it one day.

Keri is my best friend; we've known each other since we were kids. She has been the only constant in my life. I grew up in foster care, bouncing from one house to another. My schools were the only thing that stayed the same. Keri knew me from before I entered foster care. I was the daughter of a drug addicted prostitute, and rumor had it my dad was either a dealer or a rock star. Either way, I've never learned who he was.

I entered the system at the age of ten when my mother overdosed. Her pimp showed up and made a call for help, then he disappeared. That was the last time I saw her. I didn't know if she lived or died, and I didn't really care. My life in foster homes was just as bad as living with my mother. There was always abuse of one sort or another being inflicted upon me. My case worker claimed to have tried to track down my family to see if they would take me, but they made claims that they couldn't find any. They didn't even bother to try to take my DNA to run a search for my father.

The last family I lived with, the Kindal's, were the nicest of all the foster families. They have a teenage son my age and a daughter who is two years younger. They did more for me than any of the other families I was placed with. I went to live with them at the beginning of high school. They offered for me to stay and were willing to adopt me into their family. They treated me like their own, something I was so unaccustomed to before then.

With them, I flourished. I made great grades, played sports, and was even on a few committees at the high school. It was thanks to my hard work and their encouragement that I landed myself a full scholarship that allowed me to attend university. When it came to our sporting events, they took turns coming to see our games. When mine conflicted with their own children's, they chose to come to mine. Their kids understood and accepted it, treating me as if I were their own sibling, rather than just some sorry kid stuck living with them. When I kept telling my foster family not to come to my games when their kids had games, they always said, "We've seen them play for years, and as a family we want you to know that we support you, no matter what."

Keri loved my last foster family. They allowed me to be me, rather than a dirty secret, like the other families had. Keri's parents were not around much, so she grew up with someone else always caring for her. She came from a fairly well-off family in which both parents travelled for work and were rarely home. I still visit my foster family on occasion, usually for certain holidays, and Keri is always welcomed since her family is never around.

Keri and I are out letting loose, trying to have a fun night out after a stressful week. We wanted to enjoy ourselves, which is why she scored the tickets for us. Apparently, some of her coworkers had bought the tickets but couldn't go and sold them to her for cheap. I didn't care how we got the tickets, only that we are going to enjoy a band we both like. With my job, I don't get to spend as much time with Keri hanging out to blow off steam, so this is a treat for us.

Our seats are actually pretty good, ten rows from the stage. The venue is an old theatre that houses a few hundred people, and it's a full house. Of course, we chose to wear our vintage shirts from their days of working the bars. We knew we would stand out in the crowd with them on since most of the fans were sporting various shirts from their new lines.

The opener, Death Mask, is not a band we've heard of before. They aren't bad, but they are nowhere close to the talent of Twisted Tragic. We've never heard of a band that came close to the sound of Twisted Tragic, and there were plenty of goth bands out there.

All I knew was the first time I heard their music I could relate. "Last Chance", one of their first singles, reminded me of getting my last chance with the Kindal's, but it was a dark song about loving someone who was bad for you. But in my case, they weren't bad for me, but good for me.

Twisted Tragic was founded by the Black brothers, Lucius and Alucard, and Nicholai Rayne. Together, they brought in Christoph Stone and Jasper Greyson, childhood friends. Lucius and Alucard are both guitarists, Nicholai their lead singer, Christoph their bassist, and Jasper their drummer. Each member brought something unique to the band, which is why they work so well together. The talent they have is off the charts.

The brothers are six foot three identical twins with ice blue eyes, raven hair, and a tanned complexion. The only way to tell them apart is by their tattoos. Alucard has a tattoo on the right side of his neck meant to look like a vampire bite with blood dripping down, however, it looks much gorier. Articles have stated that their mother named him that after Dracula (Alucard is Dracula spelled backward). Lucius, younger by three minutes, was named after light to counter the dark name of his brother, hence the light rays coming from his favorite instrument on his upper left arm. Aside from them being the guitarists, they also write their own riffs to complement one another. I don't know what it is, but the brothers captivated me from the first moment I saw them.

Nicholai primarily writes the lyrics, occasionally with the help of Lucius. His ash blond hair and gray eyes make him stand out from the others. He is the palest of them all and stands five foot eleven. He was known to be the fun guy, always having different colors streaked into his pale hair. Rumor has it, he also had a different girl each night of the week, but I don't always believe the rumors I hear.

Christoph and Jasper write the bass riffs together while Jasper writes his own beats needed to play the drums. You rarely see these two during the shows, both of them choosing to be hidden in the background. One would say that they are shy, but it was said that they are anything but. Jasper, almost as tall as the twins, stands at six foot one, has dark blond hair, green eyes, and could have been a model rather than a rock star. Christoph is five foot ten, with dark chestnut hair, light brown eyes, and looks almost scrawny, but is known to be a good fighter.

Keri would laugh if she knew my fascination with them. All she knows is that I love their music. I want to get to know the real them, not the image they portray as entertainers. I know almost everything made available to the public about the Black brothers there is, including their recent break-ups. Rumor was that Lucius's girlfriend was cheating on him, while Alucard's girlfriend was stealing from him. Another rumor was that the girlfriends gave ultimatums of marriage and the twenty-seven-year-olds didn't want that. I was dying to know what the truth was.

Currently, the sound engineers are playing recorded music while the roadies remove Death Mask's gear from the stage. The anticipation from the crowd is at a deafening level for the band taking the stage, waiting for the same thing I am; to lose myself in music that I love. To be taken to a place where nothing matters but the music flowing through our bodies. And, of course, to drool over the insanely hot brothers.

Finally, we hear the drum beat, the one Jasper uses to warm up before their first song, "Devil of Paradise", the same one each person joins in on until Nicholai takes the mic. The vibrations from the crowd cheering penetrates the theatre, and Keri and I are no exception, both of us on our feet joining the rest of the fans. One by one the spotlights hit each of the guys. As it illuminates the brother who fascinates me the most, I scream with everything I have.

Chapter Two

TONI

At the end of the show, Keri and I wait for most of the crowd to clear out before we leave. We don't want to have to fight with everyone making a dash to the exit. Keri understands my hatred of being confined into small spaces, which is why she's willing to wait out the crowd. Our plan once we get out of the venue is to hit a bar not far from here to grab a drink.

"That was awesome!" Keri's excitement is the same as mine.

"Yeah, they've only gotten better over the last few years," I reply. "I remember the bar shows we caught. I can't believe we haven't caught more of their shows since."

"You just want a chance to drool over the Blacks," she teases as she bumps my shoulder with hers playfully.

"They're hot, what do you expect?" I laugh. "It's not like you didn't drool over your fair share of rock stars."

Little does she know I had a one night stand with one of the band members back when I was 17, before I even found out about them. Keri and I had hit a party and a certain sexy blond guy and I hooked up. We were both drunk, which doesn't excuse the fact that we fucked in one of the bathrooms. It's been a secret I've carried over the years, telling no one. Not even Keri.

"Ok, let's just head to Sublime so we can let loose and get drunk. I'm in the mood to party!"

"You're always in the mood to party, Keri, but tonight, so am I!"

As Keri and I make our way to the exit, we catch a glimpse of the guys down a hall as a door closes, most likely a staff member having gone through the door. Keri hooks her arm through mine and we continue on our way, happy that the bar is only a few blocks away, and just as close to our apartment.

Danny, the doorman at the bar, knows us as regulars and waves us through. We usually come down once a month or so, occasionally more if we can afford it. Danny only knew us because we would flirt with him just to make him smile. He gives off the badass vibe due to his job, but we could tell he was a good guy. He always made sure we were looked out for whenever we were there. I'm pretty sure that Keri knew him, but she never would admit it.

Keri and I head up to the bar to order our drinks. Sublime had once been a major hotspot but had become more of a neighborhood spot now that other dance bars have taken the clientele that came for the music. We loved that there is no real dress code, the staff is friendly, the music is great, and it isn't crowded. You have space to dance or find a spot in the back to sit.

Keri and I could have gone home to change out of our band shirts, short shorts, and Doc Martens, but we chose not to. We have limited time before last call and it would have taken longer for us to change and fix our hair and makeup than it would have to just hit the bar how we were. We were vain enough, though, to at least fix our raccoon eyes a bit.

Taking our drinks from the bartender, we

find a spot near the dance floor to see how busy it is. Finishing our drinks, we head out to the dance floor. We wave to Jay, the DJ, who we're friends with. Knowing he's here playing, we know it will be a night of older, remixed dance songs along with some newer stuff by request. Jay is one of the rare DJ's who stands out in the sea of DJ's who frequent the clubs, and he's on the circuits hitting different clubs across town and occasionally out of town too.

After a couple of songs on the floor, we head over to the bar for another round. We're so busy laughing over something funny we remembered from years ago that we don't pay much attention to anything around us. As two of the guys in front of us go to vacate a spot at the bar my jaw drops, Nicholai and Christoph grin at us and nod before moving on. They had noticed us wearing their shirts.

Nicholai's ash blond hair hung around the left side of his face, ending just below his chin. He has that straight-out-of-bed look. But I know that it's from running his hands through his sweat covered hair as he was on stage. He has a fading green streak that's mixed into his hair.

His beard draws attention to his mouth; a mouth that you knew would be sinful by the shape of his pouty lower lip. One that, if I didn't like the Black brothers, I'd wonder what it would feel like. Hell, even with liking the Black brothers I still wondered.

Christoph's chestnut hair hangs in waves to his shoulders. He has a nose ring I've never noticed before. His grin gives him a boyish, playful look. He definitely doesn't look his age; he appears to be younger. Most people claim him to be the baby of the group because of his baby face. In person he does look younger, almost carefree rather than the serious expression he wears when on stage or when doing promo stuff for the band.

"Close your jaw, Toni," Keri says, after they walk away.

"But, that was," I reply, stunned. "In the same bar as us." I could barely articulate words. If they were here, that meant the rest of the band was too. And just knowing that makes me nervous.

"Oh don't be going all crazy fan girl on them. We're here to have fun," Keri snorts as she turns to the bartender to order our drinks and shots.

I take the shot from Keri and pound it back. "Thanks." I grab my other drink. We head back toward the dance floor and find a spot to stand with our drinks. I try to forget that I'd seen part of Twisted Tragic here in the same place as us. I really wanted to try and find them and hang out with them, but there was no way I'd go alone and Keri definitely wouldn't go with me.

We hit the dance floor again and lose ourselves in the music. Music is one of the things I have always allowed myself to get lost in. As a child, it was my escape from reality, a reality that I didn't want any part of, nor do I want to remember. Even when working, I allow myself to get lost in music, it's not like it's hard to some days, considering my boss is an asshole.

When the bartender bellows last call, Keri and I head back to the bar to get our last drink for the night. While we're waiting, Keri taps my arm and nods to my other side. A quick glance shows Lucius next to me. I grin at Keri and shake my head, so she knows I'm not going to initiate anything. I'm terrified to talk to him. I don't want to come across as a babbling idiot when I know I'll never be able to form a sentence.

Lucius usually keeps his raven hair short in the back and longer on top, but he's been growing it out. My fingers itch to run through the shaggy length and mess it up even more than it already is. I was dying to know if it's as soft as it looks. His eyes are bright, a complete contrast to his dark hair. His body heat is coming at me in waves, sending my underworked libido into overdrive.

Leaning over me, Keri says, "Great show tonight. My friend and I caught it and have to admit it was better than when we caught you by chance in a bar years ago." I wanted to blush with embarrassment; she's calling attention to us and I know we look less than perfect.

"Thanks," he responds in a deep voice as he looks us over. I highly doubt we live up to their standards for girls. They've had models for girlfriends, not averagely attractive girls. "Glad you enjoyed it."

"Hey, Luc, who's the chicks?" Alucard asks as he takes in his brother talking with us.

I hadn't even noticed him come up behind us.

Alucard's hair hangs down past his shoulders. Their hairstyles show the differences in their personalities and styles, despite them wearing similar clothes. Both brothers are wearing jeans that hug their muscular legs and show off how long they are. Their shirts are tight and their muscles are straining against the fabric. Usually Alucard wears cut off shirts, baring his strong arms.

"Never caught their names, Al."

"Hi, I'm Toni, and this is my friend, Keri. We were just telling your brother that we enjoyed the show tonight compared to ones we caught when you were working the bar scene," I answer Alucard. My hands shake and my cheeks feel like they're on fire.

A look passes between the brothers, as if they were silently communicating. Lucius gives a brief nod before Alucard says, "Why don't you girls come hang out after? We've got a party going on that we need to make an appearance at."

Keri and I exchange a look. We don't have any plans for the rest of the night or the next day. My plans are mainly to catch up on sleep;

my boss has been working me pretty hard lately.

"Sure," Keri replies. She's always down for some fun, especially if it's something worth bragging about.

We order our last round and follow the guys to the back of the bar where they've been hiding from the crowd. Alucard introduces us to the rest of the band, and I have to admit that they're hotter in person than I thought. I did my best not to act like a complete awestruck fan. Secretly, I was excited because this was something I had wanted to do years ago, but was too chicken to talk to them when I first saw them play. And not to mention, I did my best to not look at the blond who I slept with before. No need to draw attention to that fact.

When we finished our drinks, we followed the guys back to a hotel. I'm giddy in my steps and excitement is vibrating through my body. One of the guys opens the door to the ballroom where, in fact, there's a huge party in full swing. There are fans, their road crew, and the media all mingling together, waiting for the band. The guys are rushed by adoring fans the moment we enter, so Keri and I slip away looking for someplace to get a drink.

Chapter Three
LUCIUS

No matter how many times we've played in front of a crowd, I always feel jittery. It's a mixture of excitement and nervousness. I know I have nothing to be nervous about; our fans love us, and being so close to our hometown, we know we have plenty of local fans here tonight. But the high we get from playing live is like no other. We never dove into the lifestyle of drugs like many other artists have. Sure, we drink a fair amount, but we never touch anything else. Heck, after a show I usually just have one drink with the guys before crashing. I'm always left exhausted after performing for hours and I'm usually the first to crash on most nights.

Tonight kicks off yet another tour for us. We've been working non-stop for the last six years, since we scored a record deal, because we wanted to make it to the top. We've had seven North American tours with seven albums released. The last four tours we've headlined rather than toured as an opener.

I have to admit that the fame that comes with being a Rockstar isn't always what we dreamed it to be. We knew about the long hours we'd be spending in studios and writing new music, but we didn't realize how much time we'd spend travelling for this or that. But we wouldn't want to change it. Sadly, the downfall is, we can't keep anything private. Mine and Al's recent break-ups have been splashed everywhere, and my ex isn't helping things.

My brother, Alucard, and I exchange looks from across the stage. We're both high from the adrenaline that comes with playing, but our bond makes it more intense as we both feel the other's excitement. As kids, we could always feel each other's emotions, but as we got older, we learned how to control it. We never understood it until we were older and learned that many times twins could feel the mental or emotional state of the other, same as an empath would. We learned that when we got lost in playing we could feel one another's emotions. It's probably why we work so well as the guitarists; we can play off one another so easily.

Our first set having finished, we've stepped off the stage to quickly down some water and dry off, while Nic talks with the crowd. He'll take his turn during the extended intro of the next song. Jas is drenched and changing his shirt; we've told him countless times to just go shirtless, but he never listens to us. Al and I usually opted to go shirtless the second half. Chris does the whole show shirtless, and Nic is hit or miss as to whether he does or not.

I glance out into the crowd as I down my water. My gaze stops when I see a pair of ladies with t-shirts from back when we worked the bars. I can't help but smirk, remembering the fun times we had back then, when we were a little more carefree. It isn't until the blonde turns to face the stage that my heart stutters.

Fuck me, it can't be her. It's been six years since I saw her at the bar before she disappeared. It's the face of the woman that has haunted me with regret for not having the balls to talk to her.

"James," I holler at the roadie. When he

comes toward me, I point to the woman and her friend. "Find those girls after the show and either get them backstage or find out where they're going, follow them if you have to."

"On it, boss," James responds. He never lets me down when I want something.

Alucard quirks an eyebrow but doesn't say anything as we relieve Nic and begin the extended intro to our newest single, "Blackened Heart". The lighting on the stage prevents me from seeing her, but that doesn't stop me from wanting to, wanting to finally talk to her.

When the show is finally over, we head off stage. Thankfully, we have another show here tomorrow so none of our stuff needs to be torn down tonight. All that is needed is the opener's stuff to be set back up. Death Mask is opening again and only travelling for our Canadian dates. We've picked up another opener for our leg in the United States.

I hand off my guitar to one of our roadies while grabbing the towel they offered to dry off some of the sweat I worked up from performing. I hope James is able to get the girls back here for me. Alucard wraps me in a headlock no sooner than I have the towel slung around my shoulders.

"So, little brother, what was up with you and James? Trying to pick some tail for tonight?"

I punch my brother in the side; it's the only way to get him to let go. He rubs his side scowling at me. "You remember that girl from that summer? I think she's here."

"The one you were too pussy to talk to? The one I would have picked up if you weren't interested in? She was pretty hot," he chuckles.

"Yeah," I reply tossing the towel onto the couch in the dressing room. "She and her friend had on the t-shirts we sold that summer to try to make some extra cash. I haven't seen one of them in years."

"What are you going to do about it," he asks.

"Do about what?" Nic asks as he dries his hair.

"Remember the summer we saved up to record our demo before we got signed? Luc was being a chicken-shit pussy about talking to that girl who showed up at every show," Alucard said, snickering, deliberately trying to provoke a reaction from me.

"Vaguely," Nic answers. "There's been a lot of girls we see, not to mention fuck."

"Well, Luc here," Al says, throwing his smelly armpit around my shoulders, "thinks he saw her in the crowd tonight. So I was asking him what he was going to do about finding his balls for once and talk to her."

I playfully shove my brother. "Fuck you, Al. I asked James to either get them back here or find out where they're going after the show."

"Nice." Nic smirks. "Going all stalker."

I give him the finger, not in the mood for their bullshit. I just want to know if it really was the girl from six years ago. I change out of my sweat-drenched clothes and into fresh ones. We'll have to wait until we're back at the hotel to shower because we have the after party we're supposed to hit soon.

Chapter Four
TONI

KERI AND I FIND A CASH BAR ALONG THE BACK wall. Ordering drinks, we try to find someplace to hang out. We're approached by a couple of girls who noticed us come in with the guys. I had to laugh when they asked about our relationship with the band and figured them to be fangirls who would throw themselves at celebrities. I wouldn't chase anyone; if they wanted me, they would have to come to me. That's probably why I'm still single. I usually make a guy work for it if he wants me.

Keri and I excuse ourselves to go get another beer. Unlike most of the girls here, we preferred beer to fruity, frou-frou drinks. After getting a new bottle, we decided to find somewhere else to stand and watch, seeing as we didn't know anyone else here and really didn't want to be talking to fake bitches.

We laughed when we see Nicholai surrounded by girls at one point, most of them in skimpy outfits, trying to get his attention. I point out to Keri when I spot my boss; it figures he would be here of all places. Keri and I work for a magazine where she's a personal assistant and I'm a research assistant.

"Guess we should go say hi to Rick," I grumble. Keri follows me as I make my way toward him. He recognizes us immediately.

"Toni, Keri. It's a surprise to see you here," Rick says, raising an eyebrow.

"Yeah, last minute invite. We were at the show and got an invite when the band showed up at the bar we went to after," Keri replies.

"You know the band?" he asks.

"Not personally. We struck up a conversation with them while waiting to be served and got the invite," I say.

"That's too bad; personal knowledge of them could be helpful for the article we'll be running next month. We have an interview set up with them tomorrow before their next show. A personal twist would be nice, however we can't seem to find their girlfriends or ex-girlfriends to get comments. And the families refuse to talk to us."

After talking with Rick for a bit longer, we decide to get another drink. But before we can make it to the bar, Alucard is beside us handing us drinks, Lucius standing not too far behind. At five foot nine I feel small next to them, and I'm sure Keri's five foot six frame feels even smaller.

"Thank you," I say, taking my drink.

"The real party is upstairs if you want to come," Alucard hints, wiggling his eyebrows up and down.

"Lead the way," I reply without looking at Keri. I don't care if she follows, I want to spend some more time with the Black brothers. Alucard scares me, and I find Lucius to be very quiet. And the way he looks at me sends shivers up my body.

We follow the Black brothers to the bank of elevators, then ride quietly to their floor. I feel a pull to Lucius that has me leaning against the wall near him. I wonder what it would be like to kiss him, to feel his skin against mine. Knowing I wanted him and acting on it are two different things, though. I can't afford to allow myself to get caught up in anything that will leave me more broken than I already am. And he has trouble written all over him.

When we step off the elevator at their floor, we find doors propped open and people milling about, mostly girls. I feel overdressed because every single girl I see is wearing a skimpy outfit.

"There's alcohol in almost all the rooms, help yourself," Alucard says as he disappears.

Keri leads the way to find something to drink, Lucius following behind. He grabs a couple bottles of beer, takes my hand, and pulls me away. He heads to a suite near the end of the hall. Leading me into the room, he continues to one of the bedrooms and closes the door.

He lets go of my hand to deposit the beer on one of the tables.

"I'm not that type of girl; one who would jump into bed with someone just because they're a celebrity." I need him to know that this will go no further than us talking.

"Then maybe I should tell you I don't sleep around with girls when I'm on tour." He chuckles. "After a show I usually just crash after having a couple of drinks with the guys. But there's something about you I'm drawn to. I felt it six years ago when you used to come see us at the bars, but I couldn't get close to you then."

"You're trying to get me to believe that you remember me from six years ago at the bars where you used to play?" I ask skeptically.

"For two whole months I was trying to get up the nerve to approach you. And when I finally decided to talk to you after one of our shows, you were gone, and I never saw you again."

"Red Deer didn't offer much for post-secondary education. I came here for school and haven't been back, aside from holidays." I look away. "What would Nikki think about me being in your room? She is your girlfriend, after all."

"Nikki and I broke up. She was cheating on me while I was away and got pregnant. I learned that she was only with me for what I could offer her. She wanted the fame that went with being connected to the band," he says with a resigned sigh.

"So, the rumours are partly true, then," I say. "Just so you know, I'm not going to be a rebound girl. I'm not here to sleep with you. I only came in hopes to get to know the real you, not the persona that you show to the world. But there's something that you need to know about me before you decide whether you let that happen."

"What could be so bad?"

"First off, I'm a research assistant for a magazine who's doing a spread on Twisted Tragic, and if word gets out I know anyone from the band personally, I'll get hounded to give details. It's bad enough my boss was downstairs and saw me come in with you and most likely leave with you. I don't want to hurt any of you by accidentally giving away any information that you would rather remain private. And second, if anything were to happen between us and someone digs into my past, it will do nothing but bring shame to you."

"Your past wouldn't have anything to do with us."

"It would if they knew I was a daughter of a drug addicted prostitute who doesn't know who her father is. Who was raised in the system after her mother overdosed. If they can get past the sealed records, they will be able to find out that I was bounced from one home to another for years." My voice trembles as I spill my horrible past.

He encloses me in his arms. "That wouldn't matter to us."

"You say that now, but what happens when it becomes a scandal? Especially when rumours are that my father is either a drug dealer or was a rock star my mom partied with." I lean my head on his chest, breathing in his masculine scent.

He pulls away from me, "I need to grab a shower. If you want to go mingle for a while you can and I'll find you after."

"Sure. When Keri is ready maybe we'll head out. You're probably tired and don't need someone hanging around keeping you awake," I say, tilting the last of the beer in my bottle.

"I didn't mean you have to leave," Lucius quickly says. "I want to spend time with you, get to know you."

"I guess she can find me when she's ready. It's not like it would be hard to find out where I went."

Lucius leaves the bedroom to take a shower. While he's gone, I fish my phone out of my pocket and check my messages.

Keri: Where are you?

Me: Drinking in Lucius's room with him.

Keri: You going to be ok? I'm in one of the rooms with a lot of people. The rest of the guys are here.

Me: I'm fine. We're just talking, that's all.

Keri: Be careful!

Me: I will.

I sit down on the king size bed and laugh to myself because I should be more worried about her. Lucius already said he doesn't sleep with girls while on tour, but I'm sure the other guys do, and Keri is an attractive girl. She's not usually picky about who she goes to bed with, as long as she has a good time.

I'm still staring at the message from Keri when Lucius returns. He's clad in only a pair of tight, black boxer briefs that leave nothing to the imagination. He's definitely well hung. I suck in a deep breath. It's then that I notice that most of his body is covered in tattoos, not just the ones we see when he's shirtless on stage. His body is toned, but not bulky. I catch a grin when my eyes reach his.

"Sorry, I didn't mean to stare," I say, looking away, blushing. "I didn't know you had that many tattoos."

"Most are covered. The guys know about all of them. Aside from them, only you and one other person has seen them," he responds with a sexy smile and a wink.

"Nikki," I reply dryly.

"Yeah, she was pissed after I got more of them done. She knew I had some and that I was planning to get more when we got together. I wasn't going to let anyone stop me from getting them."

"It's your body to do with what you want." I notice that he looks pretty tired, so I opt to change the subject. "You should probably get some sleep now." I stand to leave, and he grabs my wrist, halting me.

"Don't go." His tone has me pausing my escape.

I smile. I don't really want to go. "Only for a bit. Until you get tired enough to want to sleep. Then I'll go."

"Why don't you go take a shower? I'm sure

you want to get cleaned up some. I'll set out something for you to wear. That way if we both pass out while talking, you'll be comfortable. While you're in the shower I can get my brother to let your friend know where you are."

Rolling my eyes, but excited to spend more time with him, I nod. I head to the bathroom hoping that the main suite door is locked if he's going to be leaving me something to change into. The last thing I want is someone walking in on me.

Chapter Five
TONI

WHEN I STEP OUT OF THE SHOWER AND START to dry off, I find a t-shirt, basketball shorts, and boxers waiting for me. I guess the shorts are in case the boxers don't fit, but meh, whatever works. I didn't expect the boxers to fit when I pulled them on, but considering how tall Lucius is, his waist is narrow. Foregoing my bra, I pull the t-shirt on, and it's huge on my small frame.

As I enter the bedroom, I find Lucius typing on his phone. When he looks up, he stops typing. I can't help but bite my lip as I continue toward the bed. I sit down on the end, feeling awkward and not knowing why. Somehow this feels more intimate than being with any of my previous boyfriends, not that there were many.

We both lay our phones on the bedside

tables before turning to face one another.

"So, I guess you're the good brother and Alucard is the bad brother?" I ask.

He must have found my question amusing because he laughs before answering, and his laugh makes me smile as it sends a shiver through my body.

"Growing up as the youngest of three other brothers we were little terrors. Alexander, Damien, and Marius had nothing on us once we got big enough to fight them back. We drove our parents absolutely up the wall."

"I didn't know you had three older brothers. Your parents have a thing for goth names?"

"You could say that. We were all teased about our names growing up. But we didn't care, we liked being different. You had to have been teased for your name too."

"Yeah, a few of my foster parents thought I was a boy until I showed up. A few sent me back because they wanted a boy, not a girl. Eventually, I got over it. Having Keri helped. She stood up for me, knew my life had been hard already, even before entering foster care. Do your brothers look like you and Alucard?" I ask, trying to change the subject from my past.

"We look a lot alike, other than they're shorter than us. We all have dark hair and blue eyes. We take after our father. Our mother looks out of place when she's with us," he says with a fond smile.

"Was it hard to tell you and Alucard apart when you were younger?"

He lets out a sigh as he contemplates how to answer. "Our family could tell us apart from the beginning. As babies, our mom used to tell us that Alucard was the demanding one, whereas I was the content one. As toddlers, Alucard had no fear and got into everything; I was the opposite. For years during school, our friends couldn't tell us apart, but as we got older it was easier because of how different we tried to be from each other."

"What do you mean by how different you tried to be?"

He chuckles. "When we tried to express our different personalities. We dressed differently than each other. We tried to have different haircuts. At one point, Alucard bleached his hair, and our mom was pissed because we were only ten at the time."

"I can't picture either of you with bleached hair. I don't think it would suit you."

"It didn't. It looked horrible as it grew out. Our mom ended up buzzing his hair because of it."

Without even realizing it, we've been slowly shifting ourselves until we're closer. Lucius slips an arm under me and pulls me against his strong body. His hand trails up and down my spine, creating shivers throughout my body. My fingers trace the different tattoos on his chest as we talk. We only have a lamp beside the bed casting a muted light in the room, giving it a cozy, intimate feel. We talk a bit more about his childhood, but it isn't long before we drift off, comfortable in one another's embrace.

Chapter Six
TONI

As I start to stir, I feel a heavy weight pinned across my stomach. My eyes drift down and I find an arm around me, along with legs tangled up with mine. I almost panic when I remember I fell asleep in bed with *the* Lucius Black after talking for who knew how long. I smiled to myself, excited about the fact that I spent the night with someone I had a huge crush on.

Pulling me closer to him, I could tell Lucius was starting to stir, his erection evidence of that. I know it wasn't because of me. I know most men woke with one, so I didn't take offense to it. But I couldn't help wishing that I was the cause of it.

"I didn't fall asleep on you, did I?" asks a sleep-roughened, almost raspy sounding, deep voice. It's sexy as hell and makes my insides heat up.

"No, I think we fell asleep around the same time," I reply. "I don't even know what time it was or what time it is now."

His arm leaves me as he reaches for his phone and I suddenly feel bereft. That feeling doesn't sit well with me. As much as I like him and enjoyed the time we've spent together, I can't allow myself to get caught up with him. It will only end with me being hurt. We would never have a normal relationship, if it ever developed that far. He would always be gone.

"It's only nine, it's too early to be awake," he says, as he pulls me father into his embrace.

"I guess that's why I still feel tired," I reply, yawning.

"Go back to sleep," he says groggily, nuzzling into my hair.

I lay in his arms, eyes closed, willing myself to sleep. I can hear his soft breathing as he sleeps behind me. But sleep evades me, my mind wandering, keeping me from falling asleep again. Thankfully, I don't have plans for today or tomorrow, so I can actually catch up on sleep later. Thank God for weekends.

I must have dozed off again at some point. My eyes open to find myself curled up against Lucius's side, our legs tangled together, and my arm over his torso. Shifting, I look up at him to find him watching me.

"How long have you been awake?" I ask.

"Not long," he replies, leaning his head down to kiss me.

Stunned for a moment, in shock that he's kissing me, I finally return his kiss. My body aching for more of him, my breasts are swollen and heavy, nipples pebbled. Need is pooling between my legs, and I'm aching to be touched. I sigh, and Lucius takes advantage of my parted lips, slipping his tongue in. Allowing him to deepen the kiss, my body begs for more.

Regret fills me when he pulls away. I want more.

"Sorry, I've wanted to do that for a while now," he apologizes with a sexy rasp.

"You don't need to apologize for that," I reply. "I've wondered what that would be like."

"You have?" I could hear amusement in his voice, like he was surprised by my admission.

"Yeah. When we first caught you playing at the bar, I was attracted to you and Alucard. Probably because you're identical. That summer, I convinced Keri to come out with me every time I knew you were playing, so I could see you. I was too shy to approach either of you, and Keri had no interest; she just wanted to have fun before we left for school."

"You're telling me if my brother had shown interest in you that you would have hooked up with him?" His expression shows his displeasure at the thought of that.

"If he had, I would have learned quickly that it wasn't him who I wanted but you," I say, blushing. "Yes, I was physically attracted to both of you, but he's not the same as you. People like to think you're alike in every way, but you aren't. He's more wild than you, whereas you're more down to earth. You both have different tastes."

"Most girls wouldn't care which one of us they hooked up with, they would just brag that they did. Or they only care about what they would get out of it."

"The ones who only care about what they

get out of it are only for a good time. There are girls who aren't like that, who would want you for who you are, not what you can offer them. Those are the girls who deserve to be with you, but I doubt they can handle the lifestyle that comes with being who you are."

"Would you be able to handle it?" he asks tentatively.

"I don't know," I answer honestly. "Even though all we've done is talk and sleep, I've enjoyed spending this time with you. I could see myself falling in love with you, but I don't know how I would handle you being on tour all the time or working in the studio. We'd rarely get to see one another. How would that be fair to either of us if we tried to be together? Besides, we live in two different places."

"You could always come on tour with us. The other guys have brought their girlfriends along before. It gets crowded sometimes on the bus, but we could make it work."

"I work, I couldn't go on tour with you."

"What about when you take vacation time? I can fly you to wherever we are. We could make it work."

"I've only been there a year, so all I get is two weeks of vacation. That's not a lot of time to get together. Even if you're home, I'd only be able to come visit on the weekends unless I'm out of town. Sometimes they send me out on assignment to do research and I could be gone for weeks at a time." Sadness laces my voice at the thought.

Hope lights his eyes as he says, "We can use your job to our advantage. They want to do a personal spread on the band, right? How much more personal can you get than if you're with me? All you have to do is convince them to let you come with us. I'm sure the guys will agree to it."

"What exactly are you suggesting?"

"That we explore what it is between us," he answers. "If the guys and your boss agree to it, we could have that chance."

"You're actually serious about this?" I can hear the shock in my tone. This gorgeous, talented man wants to spend more time with me? Wants me to go on tour with them?

His eyes flash with anger, almost as if he is mad that I am resisting his offer. Or was it hurt because he thought I didn't want him that way?

"Lucius, I have trouble being in relationships with people. I didn't grow up the way normal kids do. I push people away or I become too clingy or jealous. I don't know how to be in a relationship with someone. The three relationships I've had didn't end well because of that. I don't want to hurt you." I felt the need to explain to him why I'm shocked that he'd even suggest it.

"And what, you're just too scared to even try?" he asks, anger thick in his tone.

I can feel it in the tightness of his body. I should have feared it. But I know he won't hurt me, at least not physically. Not like the foster parents I'd been shoved between had.

I sit up, pulling away from him. "I guess you just don't understand it. Why should you? You grew up in a family that obviously loved you. You learned how to deal with relationships and friendships. You knew the score, knew if you needed it, that you would have someone be there for you. You have no idea what I went through and why I don't know how to be in a relationship, let alone a friendship. Keri is my only friend."

"Then tell me, so I can understand," his tone was trying to be understanding, but I can still hear the frustration in his voice. I take a deep breath, close my eyes against the memories, and then tell him.

"My mother never wanted me. She pawned me off every chance she got so she could go sell herself to make money and spend it on drugs. She'd leave me with different people for days on end to go binge. The only reason she didn't get an abortion was because she saw me as a guaranteed monthly paycheck. When I was home with her, she was too stoned to even bother with me. I had to fend for myself to eat, and that's when she actually bothered to buy food." I take another deep breath to fight off the pain I feel when talking about her.

"When I started school all the kids used to tease me. My clothes were worn and dirty because she rarely did laundry. I had to learn real quick how to bathe myself because she never would. When she had John's coming to the apartment, I was always locked up in the closet. That was my life until I was ten, when my mother's pimp found her overdosed and I was taken away from her. The next four years found me bouncing from one foster home to the next where I was abused in one form or another. It wasn't until I started high school that I met the Kindals, who were the only family who were nice to me and let me stay with them until I graduated. They treated me like I was one of their own children. Even their own two kids treated me like I was part of the family. But I didn't know how to interact with them anymore than I know how to interact with most people. I kept them at arm's length, wondering when the rug would be pulled out from under me."

I was sitting on the edge of the bed facing away from Lucius. I try to fight back the tears staining my cheeks, angered by their betrayal. I had grown up fighting to not show anyone the emotions that came from my past. Keri being the only exception, she knows everything. I was amazed that I had been able to keep my voice steady while telling Lucius my story. A sob escapes, betraying my silent pity party.

Lucius is in front of me within moments. I hide my face in my hands only for him to pull them away before pulling me into his arms. I allow myself to seek comfort in his embrace, hoping that he doesn't feel pity for me. I hated when anyone felt pity for me; I got enough of that growing up.

When he knows I've stopped crying, he shifts enough to tip my head up to his. In his eyes I see warm tenderness before he leans in to kiss me. I should have pushed him away. I should have left before falling asleep. But whatever is drawing us together stopped me from doing what I know I should do.

I gasp when Lucius pulls me tighter against his body. I can feel him moving us as he deepens the kiss. He's shifting me on the bed and settling above me, his weight pressing me to the mattress. With a knee, he parts my legs to settle between them. His heavy erection hits the spot where I crave him the most, causing desire to ignite inside of me. I moan into his mouth when he rubs himself against me, my toes curling with the sensations flitting through me.

"This is what you do to me," he whispers against my lips, as he rolls his hips against my throbbing core. "This is what you did to me the first time I saw you. I wanted you back then as much as I want you now. I'm not always patient when it comes to something I want, but I'll try to be patient with you while you figure out if you want me as much as I do you."

Would he still want me knowing the terrible secret of me having slept with his bandmate?

"I do want you. I'm scared to want you, to have you," I admit. I can't believe that I admitted that to him. My heart's beating hard against my chest with embarrassment.

"Scared of what?" he asks softly.

"Of getting hurt. Of hurting you. Of making a mess of everything." If my secret gets out it would hurt all of us, me most of all.

"No relationship is perfect, baby. All you have to do is try."

"Ok," I whisper, hoping I'm not making a mistake.

He kisses me again with tenderness, breaking the kiss only to pull his shirt from my body before starting to explore me with his hands and mouth. When he reaches my swollen breasts, I can't help the moan that slips out when his mouth sucks in my pebbled nipple. My back arches, offering him more. Offering me.

Aroused beyond anything I have felt before, I squirm against him. One of his hands grips me by the ass as he grinds into me. I'm aroused to the point that I know I'm weeping from my opening. My clit is swollen, begging to be touched.

"Lucius," I beg, not sure what exactly I'm begging for. When Lucius pulls back, I whimper at the loss of contact.

"Fuck that's hot, seeing you in my boxers," he groans before pulling them down my legs. "But they have to go."

I let out a giggle before his mouth descends onto mine. One hand seeks lower, slipping through my wet folds, parting them and finding the bundle of nerves begging for attention. I gasp as pleasure takes my body soaring, an orgasm ripping through me. His mouth muffling my cries.

His fingers slip into my opening, stretching me. My fingers that had dug into his shoulders relaxed enough to continue to roam over his muscled back and arms.

Pulling away, he walks over to where his

wallet is sitting on the dresser. I watch as he pulls out a foiled package, and I'm silently thankful that he has protection, because I burn to feel him within me.

I stare as he shoves his boxers down his legs and returns to me. His swollen shaft rises toward his navel, thick with desire. I can only hope I'm prepared enough to take him; he's larger than my previous three boyfriends.

Climbing back onto the bed, he settles into the place he vacated moments before.

"Lucius," I beg. I don't know why I'm begging, other than for wanting him.

Ripping the package with his teeth, he makes quick work of sheathing himself. Leaning down to kiss me again he positions himself at my entrance, teasingly so.

"Lucius, please," I beg again.

He slowly starts to sink into me, advancing and retreating until I've taken all of him. His hissing grunts are the only acknowledgement of my tightness around him. He goes slowly, allowing me to adjust to his size. All I can feel is burning pain that becomes pleasure as my body accepts him. It's been so long since I've been with anyone that even I knew I was tight.

I move my hips in an attempt to take him deeper, matching him thrust for wonderful thrust. His slow, steady pace is driving me mad. "Lucius," I plead, wanting more.

He increases the speed of his thrusts. I cling to him, knowing he will take me to the bliss we both seek. I wrap my legs around his back, gasping at the position change as my hips slip upward. My pleasure building, pooling, waiting to be pushed over the edge.

My orgasm takes me by storm, coming on suddenly and crashing down on me. My whole body tenses, then I explode into a million pieces. I cry out into Lucius's shoulder before sinking my teeth into the soft flesh.

It's as if a switch is flicked. Lucius begins to power into me until he slams into me one last time, holding himself there as he lets out a grunt before slowly thrusting through the rest of his release.

"I didn't hurt you, did I?" he asks tenderly, as he brushes the ash blonde hair from my face.

"No, why would you have?" I ask breathlessly.

"You were pretty tight even with my impatient attempt at getting you ready. It's like you haven't had sex in forever."

"It's been about two years, since my last relationship," I reply. My cheeks burn with embarrassment. I hate having to admit how long it's been.

There's a loud bang on the bedroom door and Lucius curses. Slipping from my body, he quickly removes the used condom and tosses it into the garbage can before yanking on his discarded boxers. I pull the covers over me, not wanting to be seen naked. Lucius glances back to make sure I'm decent before opening the door.

Alucard looms in the door. "Fuck, Lucius, get ready. We're supposed to be doing the interview this afternoon, and we need to leave in 30 minutes. If you'd been answering your fucking phone you would know that."

I blush even more when Alucard glares at me, as if he's accusing me of being a distraction. It's like he expected me to leave when Keri left. I bite my lip and look away, suddenly unsure of what I should be doing, or if I should have agreed to try.

Lucius closes the door in his brother's face. He picks up the t-shirt I'd worn last night and tosses it on the bed. "Put that back on. We can have a quick shower to get cleaned up before we have to go."

"Why don't you go have your shower and I'll get changed to head home."

"You can have a shower with me, then we'll stop at your place along the way so you can get changed and pack an overnight bag. I want you to come with me," he says.

Letting out a sigh, I pull the shirt on and take his offered hand.

Chapter Seven

TONI

Tᴙᴜᴇ ᴛᴏ ʜɪs ᴡᴏʀᴅ, ᴡᴇ ʜᴀᴠᴇ ᴀ ǫᴜɪᴄᴋ sʜᴏᴡᴇʀ and stop at my place so I can get changed before the car service takes us to the theater where they had their show the night before. Lucius holds my hand as he leads the way backstage where the rest of the guys are waiting.

Alucard is glaring at me when we enter the room. It's like any other theater, with a wide-open backstage area that has high ceilings and tons of storage space for props and equipment. The rest of the guys are standing around talking, with Alucard facing toward where we entered. I don't know what I did to piss him off, but his attitude has changed completely since the night before. Maybe he's having a mood swing or he doesn't like the fact that his brother and I have spent all this time together. Maybe he doesn't want his brother to be with anyone, especially after how Nikki treated him.

Releasing my hand, Lucius joins the guys. My boss is staring between me and Lucius. I shift uncomfortably, knowing he will probably figure out something is going on between us and ask me about it later. The last thing I want is my boss to know what is happening in my personal life.

Christoph and Nicholai both seem to be amused, wearing Cheshire cat-like grins. Jasper looks like he doesn't even care; he looks bored. I just hope I wasn't recognized from seven years ago as a girl who had a one night stand, but I doubt he recognizes me since he never approached me at the bar six years ago. But they are talking about something, probably me, with how two of them keep sneaking glances my way and grinning. I can tell they're up to something that they aren't sharing with the others.

Alucard is still glaring at me, but his expression softens as Lucius speaks. He doesn't look happy with what Lucius must have been saying, but he respects his brother. Whatever

Lucius is saying to his brother, it looks like he's accepting it, and I wasn't sure I wanted to know what it is.

Moments later, Lucius returns to me with a grin on his face. Clearly, he was up to no good while talking to the guys, but I can't help but smile. He's attractive no matter his expression, but that grin makes my knees go weak. In most of the pictures I've seen of him he's always had a brooding, almost serious expression, or occasionally a smirk.

Taking my hand again, he leads me over to where my boss and the rest of the band are waiting. We move from backstage to a lounge area that is being used more as a dressing room. It's set up for comfort and was a little quieter than backstage where workers milled around.

I sit off to the side, watching as Rick asks them question after question for almost an hour. Most of the questions are regarding their new album and a few are personal, of which the guys try to avoid answering. I'm just glad that my boss doesn't ask Lucius about me; I want to keep that somewhat private.

As Rick starts to pack up his stuff, Nicholai

asks, "So is it true you want to have a personal spread done about us?" He gives me a quick glance with a sly grin and a wink.

"Yes," answers Rick. "But we haven't been able to reach anyone willing to talk."

"Toni is your research assistant, right?" Nicholai asks.

"Yes, she is," Rick slowly answers. He looks confused about why he's asking.

"Send her on tour with us. I'm sure she can find the answers you want," Nicholai suggests.

Christoph is grinning at Nicholai's suggestion, and I wonder why. I know the two of them have a reputation for clowning around, being the pranksters of the group. I saw it during the bar shows when they would switch the other's drinks on each other.

"I don't have the authority to make that decision. And even if I did, I wouldn't approve of it given her personal interest," he says with a smug and snide smile.

My jaw drops. "Rick, my personal life has nothing to do with it."

"It does when you spend more time fucking one of them than actually doing research. If they want a research assistant to go with them, then I'm certain we can find an unbiased one to do the job."

"I guess it would depend on how badly the magazine wants to have the spread done," Alucard threatens. "It's either her or no one. In fact, my brother dating her wouldn't get any more personal than that. We're a family, which means at some point when we make a stop in our hometown she would get to meet the rest of our family. Even if they spend time fucking, as you so eloquently pointed out, there will be plenty of time for her to gather information. You wouldn't be expecting her to be working twenty-four seven would you? So who cares what they would do during some down time."

I look at Alucard, shocked at his defense of me. He's gone from glaring in hatred at me to standing up for me. I can only assume that it's something Lucius said that has changed his attitude. Even Rick seems shocked, and maybe a little pissed off. Most likely pissed off because he'll have to give in to their demand if the higher ups actually want the story. And my boss hates when he gets overruled by anything or anyone.

He can be a prick when things don't go his way.

Before I can say anything to Rick, Lucius speaks. "It wasn't her idea, it was mine. She told me one of the reasons she shouldn't get involved with me was because of her job and what the magazine wants. I suggested it for selfish reasons. She didn't like the idea and didn't think anyone would allow it. If you're going to be an asshole, you should man up and be an asshole to someone other than a woman, especially one who's with us."

Getting up, Lucius reaches for my hand and leads me away. His body is tense with anger, so I don't say anything. The last thing I want is his anger directed at me. I'm surprised when he leads me back outside to the waiting car. I'm even more surprised when Alucard gets in the vehicle with us, appearing just as angry.

Lucius wraps an arm around me, anchoring me to him. I lay my head on his shoulder and he starts to relax. I don't get why he and his brother are so mad in my defense. My boss was right in a way; they don't want research assistants to be personally involved with the subjects, and I'm already treading too deep into that territory. But this is six years in the making. From the first day I saw Lucius and Alucard, I knew I wanted them, Lucius specifically even though it was unknown at the time.

"Where are we going?" I ask quietly, as I trail a hand up and down Lucius's arm absentmindedly.

"We have about three hours before the show starts. That means we have about two hours to ourselves. I want to take you out for dinner, but highly doubt we'll have time, so we're just going to order room service from the hotel," Lucius says. "Neither of us have eaten today since we slept most of the day. We usually take some down time before we have a show, try to get soundchecks done early so we can relax before we have to perform."

"Ok," I reply quietly and snuggle in closer to him.

When the car pulls up to the hotel, Alucard gets out first. Lucius grabs my bag from the floor and takes my hand. In the afternoon light the hotel looks different than it did last night, not that I was paying any attention at the time. The lower level of the hotel houses a number of different storefronts. Several floors are built to look modern with floor to ceiling windows before taking on the high-rise style construction. The main entrance brings you into a wide hallway until you come to the lobby, which sports a lounging area and the front desk. To the right of the front desk is another hallway leading to the bank of elevators that takes us to their floor. Once on their floor, I notice that Alucard enters a different room. I had thought that they shared a room.

Lucius lets us into the room we shared last night and then heads toward the bedroom to drop off my bag. As distracted as I was the night before by Lucius, I finally take in the room. As soon as you enter the two bedroom suite, a small, but functional kitchenette is to the left with an equally small dining area that seats four. This opens into a living area with a pull-out sofa, a chair, and a functioning workstation. The two rooms are divided by the tiles from the kitchenette and carpet of the living area. Like many hotels, an entertainment stand holds a TV, and lamps are scattered around the room despite the outside wall being nothing but a window that spans half the length of the room. Across from the kitchenette is an archway opening into a hall that leads to the bedrooms. To the right of the archway is a bedroom that I assumed was Alucard's. Straight ahead of the archway is a door that might be a closet. To the left is a small hallway that leads to the second bedroom with the bathroom right before it; this is Luc's room. I assume both rooms have a TV mounted to the wall in the corner. All the decorations are the standard scenery pictures that you'd expect to find in a hotel, nothing unique or original.

I pick up the room service menu and take a look. When Lucius enters the living area he calls down our order. As starved as I am, I hunger for something else more. As I watch Lucius move about the room, I can't help but admire the way his body moves, knowing full well the power it wields. I remember how easy it was for him to lift me, to hold himself above me as he teased me, as he made love to me.

"Keep looking at me like that and neither of us are going to be eating," Lucius says, bringing me back to reality from the memory I'd been replaying. "What are you thinking of?"

"You," I reply, looking away bashfully. "Remembering this morning, afternoon, whatever time it was."

Standing before me, he tilts my head up and leans down to kiss me. Rising on my toes, I wrap my arms around his neck and kiss him back. When he lifts me, I instinctively wrap my legs around his waist. I feel my back hit the wall as he continues to deepen the kiss.

We break apart, breathless at the sound of a knock on the door; the room service delivery. His hardness is pressing against me and my soaked thong clings to my skin, making my pulse beat erratically as I groan at the interruption. Lucius opens the door for our food delivery. I watch as the staff gets things ready for us before disappearing.

"Hurry up and eat," Lucius orders in a deep rasp, "I need to be inside you."

I lick my lips at the thought and his eyes darken with need and desire. I wanted that more than anything as well. I sit at the table beside him as we eat our food. Luc ordered a burger and fries while I opted for a pasta dish, snagging the occasional fry from his plate. The sexual tension is thick between us as we anticipate what's to come when we finish our meal.

Lifting me from the chair when we're finished and cradling me against his chest, Lucius makes his way to the bedroom. Setting me down on the carpeted floor long enough for him to strip us both, he tosses a condom package on the bed before gently lowering me. The king sized mattress soft against my back, the cover from the freshly made bed feels like cool silk against my heated skin. The muted afternoon sunlight shining in from the window allows me to watch Lucius. Wanting to make sure I am ready to take him, he focuses himself between my legs. Licking, sucking, nibbling, and stretching me with his fingers. The beginnings of his five o'clock shadow tickles my skin as he moves. His fingers curl inside me, searching for the spot that's guaranteed to make me explode for him. The calluses on his fingertips cause more friction than I thought could be possible.

Soft sighs and moans can be heard coming from me. The pleasure he is giving me is beyond what I'd experienced with him earlier. My legs shake, hips buck against his mouth.

"Lucius," I cry, as I fall over the edge into an orgasm that lasts for what feels like forever.

Beyond sensitive after his continued onslaught, I beg him to stop. I can't take anymore, I need him to fill me. Reaching for the condom, he quickly covers himself before easing into me. Knowing we don't have much time, I know this will be quick. His thrusts are deep and powerful, yet gentle. Meant to send us both over the edge rapidly.

My orgasm crashes through me before I even realize it's upon me. I'm unaware of anything going on around me other than the euphoric pleasure coursing through my veins. Stars dance across my vision, blocking the sight of the man who's brought so much pleasure to me in such a short amount of time. A man I was surely falling for.

As I blink into awareness, I find Lucius staring down at me, an amused smile on his face. "We have enough time for a quick shower before we need to leave for the show tonight," he says, as he leans down and gently kisses me.

My groaning protest earns me a chuckle. "Can I just stay here and sleep?" I ask, yawning.

"No," he replies. When I pout, he continues, "There'll be no security here, so if someone does get into the room, there won't be anyone here to help you. You can always lay down in our dressing area."

I drag my tired body into the bathroom for a quick shower. He's right, no one would be here to help me if something were to happen. Crazy fans have broken into hotel rooms before, and who's to say they don't have any crazy fans.

Chapter Eight

TONI

BEING BACKSTAGE IS CERTAINLY A DIFFERENT experience. When we arrive at the venue, a waiting crowd outside goes crazy at the sight of the guys. As I look around, I see girls openly glaring at me when they see my hand clasped by Lucius's. I can only wonder what they're thinking, or if they have the pang of jealousy I use to get seeing pictures of him and Nikki, even Sarah before her.

The guys stop and sign a couple of autographs and pose for pictures before continuing their trek inside. I can't help but admire that they would take a few moments of their busy schedule to make some fans happy. But without happy fans, they wouldn't be successful. I'm going to have to get used to seeing girls try to hang off Lucius while he's on tour.

I'm more than surprised to see Rick still milling about backstage as we walk toward the dressing area the band is using. I ignore him and allow Lucius to wrap an arm around me. He leaves a kiss on my temple before heading to get ready.

I take a seat on one of the couches and pull my phone out. I don't have any messages from Keri, but I briefly filled her in when we stopped at the apartment earlier. I watch as the guys get ready. I had figured there was a stylist who helps them, but was surprised to see there isn't. The six of us are the only ones in the room; the door closed so that no one will disturb them.

As I watch them get ready, they act as if I'm not even there, with the exception of the odd glance from Lucius. They joke and tease each other. Alucard is right, they act like brothers. It makes me sad that I never had that bond with anyone, even Keri. The family I could have had that bond with I've kept at arm's length to keep myself from being hurt and let down. And yet, I have wanted that family bond so badly.

On my phone I open the email app and do what I should have done years ago. I pour myself into the email.

Hey, guys,

I'm sending this as a group email because it's easier to express what I need to each of you. The last twenty-four hours have been different for me. I've had my eyes opened to see things in a new way. When you took me in, you knew about my past, but that didn't stop you from accepting me into your family; from loving me. I can only imagine the hurt I must have inflicted by not showing that love in return, or showing my acceptance and happiness to be part of the family. I'm sorry for any pain I have caused you because of that.

Jessica - I wish I had been the big sister you deserved to have, and for not being that for you, I'm truly sorry. I want to be a big sister you can be proud of. One who can be there for you when you need it, whether it's for a shoulder to cry on or even just to talk about guys. I want you to know that I am proud to have you as my sister. I'm proud of how far you have come from the bratty pre-teen I saw you as when I first came to live with you. Even though I never said it, you were the first person in the family I loved because of your continued pestering to get me to open up. I missed that pestering when you stopped; when you gave up on me. I vow to you that I will be the sister you deserve. You'll have to forgive me when I make mistakes, because I know I'll mess up sometimes.

Dean - I wish I could have been the sister to you that Jessica was. I wish I had let you push me into the things you found out interested me. I wish that we'd have studied together like we should have. I wish that I let you be the big, scary brother you wanted to be. I'm glad that you did stand up for me when you saw how the other kids were treating me at school; it was something that made me love you as the brother you tried to be. You did more for me than anyone else ever had, with the exception of Keri. I know I'll screw up, but I will do all I can to earn the position of being your sister.

Mom and Dad - I know it must have been hard taking a troubled teen into your home, especially one like me who had a rough go at life before you. I know you did everything you could to make me feel welcome and part of the family, even going as far as adopting me and giving me your family name. I cannot express my gratitude for the gift you gave me, the gift I didn't realize I had been given until now. I know I never said it before, so I will say it now: I love you both. I was scared to love you because I was terrified that you would be taken from me. I want to be worthy of the title of daughter and to make you proud. I want all of you to be the family I wanted but refused to believe I could have.

Love always,

Toni

Smiling to myself, I know that my family will be shocked with my new revelation. It may even take time for it to sink in with them. The only thing holding me back from happiness is myself, and I'm going to change that starting now. If all I can have with Lucius is short spurts of time, then so be it. Any time spent with him will be worth the cost of a broken heart if we can't make it work. It's worth it because he's showing me how to live again. I feel happier than I ever have. It's like a weight has been lifted from me, one that had left me feeling smothered for so long.

I glance toward where the guys are still getting ready. I swallow, my mouth and throat suddenly dry at the sight of Lucius. His hair styled into messy spikes makes me want to run my fingers through it, making a bigger mess.

His expression is serious as he and Nicholai talk. The black muscle shirt is stretched across his back, no doubt it will be the same against his chest. His black jeans make his already long legs look longer and they hug his backside perfectly, making my hands itch grab him.

I'm drowning in the desire I feel for this man. I want to rip every piece of clothing from his body and take him right here, right now. I want him to make me fly with the pleasure only he has been able to bring to me. My previous boyfriends didn't compare because they were never the one I truly wanted.

Chapter Nine
TONI

I'M WATCHING THE SHOW FROM BACKSTAGE, which is a whole other experience, one I will never forget. I have an up close and personal view of the guys playing. And it is spectacular. Every now and then Lucius glances my way and winks. He probably knows how hot I am for him right now. All I want is for the show to be over, and to be back in the hotel room in his arms. We don't have to be making love, just being held by him is good enough.

Even if we've only spent less than twenty-four hours together, I know that I'm falling for him, and falling hard. It just feels right.

I nearly jump when my phone starts to buzz in my back pocket. I pull it out and make my way toward the dressing area.

"Hello?" I answer.

"Toni, it's Mitch. I had a talk with Rick about Twisted Tragic."

Holy shit. My boss's boss is calling me. Mitch is one of the managers higher up at the magazine, and is a very personable guy. "I didn't think that he would even call you about that."

"He wants the story. I've checked their concert dates. The deadline we're hoping to make for the article won't be something we can hit if we don't agree to send you out. We might be able to push it back some, but it will be close. If we send you, you'll get paid your normal salary, plus expenses. However, you will need to submit copies of the receipts in order to be reimbursed. I'm going to assume your transportation will be with the band, but if it's not, then you won't be going."

"I can talk to the guys once the show is over and get back to you."

"Call me back right away. They have a show tomorrow, so the decision has to be made as soon as possible."

"Ok," I reply, as Mitch hangs up. Seems like Mitch is more receptive to this idea than Rick was.

I smile to myself, excited that it's a possibility that I'll be able to spend more time with Lucius than I expected. We'll be able to strengthen our bond before we'll have to be separated. Plus, I love to travel and see new places. It'll just suck that I can't be a normal tourist. Usually, I take a day or two and do tourist things wherever I go.

Arms slide around me from behind and a warm mouth nibbles at my neck. I know it's Lucius without looking. I know the feel of his lips on my skin, the way it tingles when he touches me.

"You look happy," he says.

"I am, but I could be even happier, depending on what happens after talking to you and the guys," I say, as I turn in his arms to wrap my arms around his neck, offering my lips for a kiss.

The kiss is over sooner than I'd like, but I know he's tired and probably wants to have a shower and go to bed. Sweat soaks his shirt and dampens mine where our chests are pressed together, but I don't care. The sweat isn't a turn off, but more of a turn on. I can only imagine it's because I now associate that smell on him with sex.

"Keep looking at me like that and I won't wait till we're back at the hotel to take you," he jokes. "But seriously, what do you want to talk to us about?"

"One of the higher ups at the magazine called me. They spoke to Rick earlier about your suggestion of me coming on tour with you to cover the story. They're seriously considering letting me go. However, they have one concern about my expenses, since obviously I'll still be doing my job as much as I can while spending time with you," I say.

"What are their concerns?" he asks.

"They'll cover my food expenses, which is a given anyway. They'll cover as low as they can for accommodations, but they won't cover transportation. They'll only consider sending me if I'm travelling with you, on the band's dime."

He smiles. "Well, they won't have to worry about spending money for accommodations either because most of the time we stay on the bus. The only time we stay in a hotel is if we're doing back-to-back shows in the same town. And even if we do stay in a hotel, you won't be needing your own room because you'll be sharing mine. The bus itself has six bunks and a bedroom. Usually, we take turns using the bedroom, with the exception of Nicholai and Christoph hijacking it after a show to get laid by random fans. Either way, I'm sure the guys won't care if we take it over. Their stuff will have to be stored in there, though, since there's not much for storage space when you live on a bus."

"So, you won't mind me being around you all the time?" I ask, unsure.

"We won't have as much alone time as you would think; we'll be with the rest of the guys the whole time."

"Are you sure they'll be ok with it?" I'm curious as to how I'll be able to spend a month hiding my secret. I may have to talk to him about it before I confess to Luc. Maybe if I talk to him, we can forget about it altogether and put it behind us, so it won't be awkward. Then I won't have to confess to Luc at all.

"Nicholai and Alucard wouldn't have

suggested it if they didn't agree with the idea. They want the exposure it can bring, but they also want to see me happy. They saw how I was after you disappeared on me six years ago, and knew how badly I wanted to meet you."

I can't help but grin. "Then I guess I better call him back and tell him the advantages that being with you will bring."

"I'm going to get changed before we head back to the hotel. I guess we'll have to stop at your place for you to pack."

While Lucius gets changed, I quickly call Mitch back and advise him that I won't need the expenses for hotels and that I will be travelling with the band. He authorizes me to go for one month with the conditions that I provide a regular report and that at the end of the month a review will be conducted to decide if I stay on with the band or if I'm booked to return home. A month is better than nothing.

"Are we going back to your place for you to pack?" Lucius asks.

Pulled out of my thoughts by the question, I hadn't realized that he had snuck up on me. "Yeah," I reply. "I get a month for now, and before the month is up they'll decide if I stay longer or have to head home."

Taking my hand, he leads me out to where the cars are waiting behind the building. Thankfully, we get to use the back entrance this time rather than the front. Before getting into the car I spot a bus with a trailer hitched to it and I wonder what it's going to be like living on a bus for the next month or so.

At my place I have trouble trying to figure out what I should pack. Normally when I'm going out on assignment I have no problem deciding what I need, but I secretly hope that Lucius and I will get some time to ourselves and maybe go on an actual date rather than be cooped up on the bus or in a hotel, so I don't know if I should pack some fancier outfits or not.

I pack my notebook into its carrying case, knowing I'll need it, along with several flash drives, my tablet, and my digital cameras. Knowing my hockey bag likely won't fit through the aisle on the bus, I pull out a couple of my smaller duffel bags. The first things I make sure to pack are my toiletry bags and makeup.

Lucius sits on my bed, leaning against the headboard, his big body dominating the space. The king-sized beds at the hotel allow him to sleep without having his legs bent, so my double will not be very comfortable for him. He probably needs a California King bed to sleep comfortably.

As I begin rooting through my underwear drawer, I hear a groan. Glancing at Lucius, I can tell he likes the idea of the lacy thongs I started tossing on the bed near my bags because he's adjusting the bulge at his groin. I smile to myself knowing he's picturing me wearing them, and it gives me a rush of satisfaction knowing that he desires me.

When I have everything that I think I'll need laid out on the bed, I slowly start packing it all into the two duffel bags. I just hope I have enough packed and haven't forgotten anything.

Lucius takes my two duffels while I grab my computer bag, and we head down to the waiting car that will take us back to the hotel. I'm surprised when we stop at a drugstore, but figure that he's stocking up on protection since we know we'll be having plenty of sex.

When we get to the hotel, we head straight to our floor. A couple of the doors are propped open, something I found they do so they can visit each other without having to knock on doors. I can hear laughter coming from one of the rooms and assume the guys are hanging out, joking around.

No sooner than the door to the hotel room clicks closed, Lucius drops my bags from his hands, then takes the one I'm holding and sets it down, before pinning me to the door. The hungry kiss he gives me leaves me leaning into him as desire courses through my body. I start tugging at his shirt, wanting to feel his chest beneath my hands.

Stepping away, he yanks his shirt off along with mine before pulling me into his arms again. As he kisses me, I can feel him maneuvering us toward the bedroom. Somewhere along the way I lose my bra. I struggle with getting his belt unbuckled before getting his pants undone. I can feel his erection beneath my fingers as I slip a hand into his boxer briefs to stroke his hard cock.

When the backs of my knees hit the bed,

we tumble onto it in a tangle of limbs without breaking the kiss. Lifting me with ease, he moves us up the bed. I gasp for breath as his lips move to my neck. My back arches as his soft lips trail farther down. And I moan as he takes a pebbled nipple in his mouth.

"Lucius," an angry feminine voice calls out.

Pulling away from me, we both look in the direction the voice came from. Standing almost naked near the bathroom doorway is a woman. I recognize her, but my lust-filled brain cannot place her. I can't believe whoever she is has the nerve to be here in only a pair of skimpy underwear. I'm even more horrified that she sees us in our half naked state.

"Nikki, what the fuck are you doing here?" he growls, as he moves to hide me from her.

"I came to see my boyfriend," she says.

"We broke up, Nikki," he says, his tone sounding angry. "You have no right to be here. How the fuck did you get in my room?"

"I told the nice young man at the front desk I was your girlfriend here to surprise you before you leave tomorrow. And you don't get to break up with me, Luc, especially not after my father made you who you are. And you certainly don't get to fuck around with sluts like her," she says, glaring at me.

"The only slut I see is you," he says, voice laced with anger. "You don't get to tell me who I get to be with. And I certainly don't want to be with a cheating bitch like you. You don't get to use your father as a way to try to keep me with you either. I already talked to him, told him what happened and that I left you after finding you in our bed with another man. Your father actually said that you don't deserve me if that's what you've been doing. Now, get your clothes on and get the fuck out before I have security escort you out in all you have on now."

"You wouldn't dare," she spits, her anger attempting to call his bluff.

Reaching over to pick up the phone beside the bed, he punches in a room number. "Alucard, send security over to remove Nikki... She conned the front desk into letting her up here." After hanging up the phone he turns to Nikki. "One way or another you are leaving. And I'm sure my girlfriend won't appreciate you stalking me."

Nikki looks from him to me, her angry glare definitely attempting to drill holes into me. I glare back at her for ruining this evening for us. I know she's livid because she isn't getting her way; isn't getting the man she wants back. The man she's using for her own purposes.

Lucius picks up a shirt from the side of the bed and hands it to me without looking. I don't know if it's to hide the state of undress I'm in or if it's because of how angry he is that his ex showed up. Not sure what else to do, I pull the shirt on.

I can feel the fury rolling off Lucius in waves. I'm just glad I'm not the one his rage is directed toward. Angry Lucius looks scary. I can hear the main door to the suite slam closed and I know someone is here to remove Nikki from our room.

Behind her, Alucard and two other guys I don't recognize step into view. Alucard curses. "Nikki, get dressed."

"Al, surely you won't throw me out after coming all this way to see my boyfriend," she says sweetly.

"Nikki, he caught you cheating on him.

How would you expect him to stay with you after that? I'd have left your sorry ass too! Have some respect for yourself, get dressed, and get out of here."

I know she is glaring at Alucard, but my focus is on Lucius. His body is tense and I know the moment we were having is over. As scary as both brothers can be when angry, I know that neither of them would hurt a woman. A man maybe, but not a woman. I sigh and know that tomorrow will be a new, adventurous day.

Part of me wants to go to Lucius and wrap my arms around him. But the part of me that fears his anger keeps me from doing so. It's sad how my childhood has shaped me into fearing people when they're mad.

Ignoring Nikki, I climb off the bed, walk to the window, and stare outside. I can see the city lit up around us. I wonder why Nikki bothered showing up and why her father has anything to do with the band. I wonder why she would want to cheat on Lucius. The man is a gifted musician and certainly amazing in bed, not that I have much experience in that department. I also know that Lucius is a good man, not someone who deserves to be treated like garbage.

Turning from the window, I finally notice the room is empty. I can hear the shower running as I step into the hallway leading to the living area. I grab my bags from the door where they were dropped and take them to the bedroom. I find my charger and make sure to plug my phone in. I change into a pair of shorts and then climb into bed.

Chapter Ten
LUCIUS

To say I'm furious would be an understatement. Nikki found her way into my room. And to call Toni a slut? I'm pretty sure Toni would never think about cheating on me like Nikki did. And to tell me she's pregnant? It doesn't look like she is for someone who's supposed to be four or five months along, considering I dumped her ass three months ago. I'm terrified at the idea of her being pregnant with my kid; her conception date puts it around the time we were home writing our newest album and she'd come to stay with me.

I dumped her as soon as I caught her fucking another man. Needless to say, she didn't take it well. I had to sell my house and buy another one just to get away from her. She's hounded my family ever since to find me. I even changed my phone number. I figured she got the point that I was done with her. I never expected her to show up here, dressed the way she was.

Toni was withdrawn when Nikki was finally removed from the room. She didn't deserve me taking out my anger on her, so I figured a shower would help cool me down.

Stepping from the bathroom, I find her fast asleep in bed. I smile to myself seeing her ash blonde hair spread out around her, how peaceful she looks in her sleep. I can't help but stand in the doorway admiring her.

"Luc," Al's voice calls out.

Turning toward my brother's voice, I see him wave me over. Grabbing a pair of jeans, I pull them on before following him out to the main room. "What?"

"Meet me in Chris and Nic's room. I'm getting Jas over too. We need to talk about how to deal with this shit."

"Yeah, I don't need this shit around Toni," I say, as I check to make sure I have my key card before following Al out of the room.

We find Jas leaning against the wall waiting for us, as if he knew to expect something after me calling his room to ask him to get my brother so we can have security help remove the woman I've come to despise. A woman I have no idea what I saw in that attracted me to her in the first place.

Al knocks on Nic and Chris's door. Chris opens the door, rolling his eyes when he sees us. "Now's not a good time," he says, before starting to close the door.

Al shoves the door open more, causing Chris to stumble back a little. "Now is a good time. We need to talk," Al says, as he pushes his way in.

We find two girls in the room, one of them sitting on Nic.

"What the hell?" asks Nic with a pissed off voice.

Al points at the girls as he says, "Get the fuck out. Now!"

Did I mention my brother can be an asshole and scare people? I'm sure the girls are scared, they leave the room quickly without looking back.

"What the fuck, Al?" Chris says.

"We need to talk. And no, it can't wait

till morning," Al replies, his tone not one to question.

"What's up?" Jas asks.

Al looks to me. Fuck, he's going to make me speak. "Nikki got into my room tonight."

"What?" Nic, Chris, and Jas all say at once.

"Yeah. Toni and I had just gotten back from her place so she could pack to come with us. Nikki managed to get a key card to my room from the front desk by spouting off that she's my girlfriend here to surprise me. She was practically naked, finding me and Toni making out. I had Al get security to remove her because I wasn't going to leave Toni with Nikki."

"Unbelievable," exclaims Nic. "Why the fuck would she show up now? You broke it off with her a few months ago."

"She probably figured I've cooled off enough to take her back. She planned to try to seduce me guessing by how little she was wearing. I guess she didn't get it by me moving and changing my number," I say with a tired sigh and a shrug.

Al adds, "She shouldn't have been able to get a key card from the front desk in the first place. We leave in the morning to head to the next venue; who's to say that another fan won't pull the same shit. This is a breach of security that we need fixed now, not later. And we need to talk to both our manager and the executives with the label."

"Fuck," bites out Chris. "Like we need this shit now."

"I'll start to check to see if I can find out if Nikki is posting shit on social media," Jas replies. "I just need to get my computer."

I don't know how long we spend with our security team going over plans on how to prevent this from happening again. And with it being so late, Nic is going to deal with our manager and the executives in the morning.

I can't wait to go to bed so I can curl up with my girl, but this shit needs to be taken care of first. Sure, our mood was ruined, but I can't let Toni get hurt by our flaws in security. The few that stay with us on tour can only handle so much, and we can't rely on local security to pull extra time by having them stay to watch the hotels when we stay in one.

We have five men who make up our security

team, each of them professionals with plenty of experience. They've been with us since the first time we toured, when we were virtually nobodies. Each man is assigned to one of us but work together to protect us all. When out for public appearances they work as a well-oiled machine.

At least we don't need to have security when we're home. Nor when we can get out to explore if we attempt to not bring attention to ourselves. Yesterday at the bar we had security with us; we couldn't chance it and they made sure to blend in. You never know what can happen if a bunch of drunks recognize us.

Chapter Eleven
TONI

FEELING LIKE THERE'S SOMETHING WRONG, I'm pulled from my sleep. I didn't even realize that I had drifted off. The spot next to me is empty and doesn't look like it's been slept in. I check the time on my phone to see that it's the middle of the night, the red digits blinking an angry one thirty.

Concerned, I get out of bed and head out to the main living area of the hotel room. He's not there, not in the other bedroom either. I would text him, but I don't have the number, nor do I know what room number his brother is in. With a sigh, I grab a pillow and lay on the couch, waiting for him to return.

Nikki showing up must have really done a number on Lucius. If he got upset enough that he didn't want to be around me when she showed up, then maybe we shouldn't even bother trying. Maybe I should walk away now, before I get hurt; before I hurt him with the knowledge I'm hiding. However, this new assignment won't allow for me to do that. I'm effectively trapped into a month of being around Lucius, knowing that both Nikki and I can come between us. That maybe he's still in love with her and I'm just the rebound girl.

Frustrated for allowing myself to even care about him, I start to pack the few things of mine that I have here, mostly the clothes throughout the suite. To hell with the assignment; if I get fired I'll just have to look for a new job. In the desk I find a pad of paper and a pen. Sitting down, I decide to write a note.

Lucius,

I'm sorry, but I can't do this. I know I promised to try, but I know it won't work. If we continue I'll only get hurt or I'll hurt you, and that's not something I can afford to allow to happen to either of us.

You disappearing tonight after Nikki's unexpected visit leads me to believe that you may not be over her, and I won't come second to anyone. After the life I have had, I deserve to have someone put me first, and with you I will always come after the guys, the band.

You deserve to be with someone who can accept that and who isn't damaged like me. I will treasure the moments we've had, and as brief as our affair has been, I can honestly say it meant more to me than any of the relationships I've ever had.

I'm sorry,

Toni

I leave the note on his pillow and head down to the lobby with my bags. The front desk clerk calls a cab for me and I sit outside to wait. With the late hour, it doesn't take long for the taxi to arrive to take me home. I make it all the way to my apartment before I break down in tears on my bed.

I try to convince myself that walking away is the best thing, but it hurts to leave him. I've only spent a short time with him, so why does it feel like I've left a part of me behind? I couldn't possibly care for him as much as I feel I do.

I'm glad to discover that Keri is out. The last thing I want is for her to be trying to find out why I'm so upset. She would most likely tell me I'm blowing things out of proportion. Maybe I am, but she doesn't know about the fact that because of her, I slept with one of the band members before. I never thought that night could come back and haunt me. It was just supposed to be a onetime fuck, can't even call it a one-night stand since I didn't spend the night, seeing as how we fucked in a bathroom at a party.

I fall into an exhausted sleep, crying, repeating, "It's for the best" to myself. It truly is for the best that I forget about Lucius Black. Nothing but heartache can come from anything that ever happens between us. I can treasure our time together as a fun experience without the damper of anything to darken my memory of him.

Chapter Twelve

TONI

An unfamiliar alarm pulls me from my sleep. I let out a groan knowing it's far too early to be awake, especially after crying myself to sleep so late at night. As my mind begins to clear, I register a weight at my waist. Looking down, I see an arm possessively holding me, a very familiar arm. An arm belonging to the reason I cried myself to sleep: Lucius.

As the arm moves, the warmth at my back disappears. The alarm stops and then I'm pulled farther into his embrace.

"Why did you leave?" His voice has that sexy, sleepy rasp.

"Because I can't do this," I reply honestly, while trying to gently untangle myself from him. But he doesn't let me.

"Can't do what?" he asks, while pulling me

closer and tightening his hold on me.

"I can't be with you without one of us getting hurt." And I don't want to hurt him.

"I think you've made an assumption that's clearly wrong, and maybe that's my fault. When Nikki left, you were lost in your thoughts, so I went to have a shower because I needed to calm down. When I got out of the shower, you were already asleep and Alucard wanted to talk with all of us as to what we needed to do about Nikki, so what happened last night won't happen again. I should have let you know where I was, but I didn't expect you to wake up. And we should have had each other's cell numbers so you could have messaged me or I could have messaged you when I found you gone."

"How did you get in?" I ask, puzzled.

"Keri. She arrived just after I got here. I told her what happened, she rolled her eyes and let me in. I found you sound asleep, so I figured I might as well let you rest."

"Why was Nikki throwing around her father's name?"

He sighs before answering, "Her dad's one of the executives with the record label. She figured her dad would threaten to drop us if I didn't stay with her. However, that's not the case. Nicholai is going to call him today and tell him that if Nikki doesn't stop her antics, things will get a little ugly with us pressing harassment charges against her. I've already had to change my cell number because of her constant calling me and she's shown up at the rest of my family's places looking for me because I sold my house and moved. If I had known how much trouble she'd cause, I wouldn't have gotten involved with her."

"This still won't work with us," I say sadly.

"Why do you say that? How do you know if you don't try?"

"You'll be gone all the time. I won't be able to spend any quality time with you because even if I did fly out to where you are, you will be working most of the time."

"You don't know that. Come with us and see how it can be. Or you can quit your job and we can be together."

"You wouldn't be happy with someone who doesn't work. You don't want to be responsible for supporting someone you're with."

"I can always talk to the guys to see if they want to hire you to handle all of our social media. Right now, Jasper handles as much of it as he can, but he can't keep up with all of it. You've got cameras, so you can post pictures of us, and I'm sure being around us, you can answer the questions from our fans. It wouldn't be that hard, and I know Jasper would love not having to do it all the time."

"Eventually you'll get sick of me being around all the time, and I can't leave Keri to fend for herself here." That and I'm pretty sure if word gets out that I slept with another band member it will make things awkward.

"You won't have to, we'd pay you. You can take pictures during the concert, and while we're travelling you can upload them at any time. It's the easiest way for us to be together so that you don't feel like you're coming in second all the time. You can think about it and make a decision when the magazine decides they want you to come back. You can send them whatever they need for the article and then stay on with us."

"How about I try doing that, along with

what the magazine wants me to do for the month they're letting me go? It will give me time to decide what I want to do. It will be the only way I will know if I can spend that much time travelling. Or if the guys get sick of having me around."

Pulling me close, he nuzzles my neck, "Good. Get up. We have to go catch the bus, and the car should be here to get us soon. I arranged for it to come back after I got dropped off. We can get some more sleep on the bus."

Getting up, I head to the bathroom to get ready. Thankfully, knowing I can sleep some more eases my mind when I see the black circles under my eyes. They're still a little puffy, but any redness from crying is gone. Knowing we'll hopefully be going back to sleep, I choose not to put makeup on.

Back in my room, I look through my closet for something to wear. I opt to keep on my tank top but add a bra. I exchange my shorts for a pair of sweats and make sure to change my underwear so that it matches the bra I'm wearing. Of all things, I always try to make sure my underwear matches, even if my clothes don't.

We gather my bags and leave. As promised, the car is waiting to take us back to the hotel. When we pull up to the back of the hotel, their bus is sitting near the exit. The bus looks small from the outside, no bigger than a greyhound bus, making me wonder how they live for months on end in such a cramped space. The shiny black and silver is a contrast to their matte black and silver TT logo. You'd miss their logo if you didn't know to look for it; it was probably done to not draw a lot of attention to them when travelling.

Lucius leads the way to the bus. Stepping on, I find that as small as it looks, it's actually fairly spacious. There's a seating area with a galley kitchen at the front. Beyond that is a curtained off area that leads to six bunks, three stacked across the aisle from each other. As we pass the bathroom, I'm a little curious about how open it is before hitting the bedroom.

We drop my bags on the bed and Lucius leaves to get his own stuff from the hotel room. Curiously, I start to look around the bus a bit. I stand in the area that is supposed to be the bathroom and wonder how I will shower with five guys being able to walk in at any time.

"You just have to warn us so we can make sure to give you some privacy," Alucard says, startling me. "We're not complete jerks who won't allow you privacy. Us guys usually don't care about seeing each other naked. Until you've been around us long enough to not care, we won't be assholes."

Blushing, I reply, "Thanks. I didn't think the bathroom would be so open."

"I give it two weeks before you start being comfortable enough around us to not warn us. We're guys, of course we'll look, but it doesn't mean we'll be trying to take you to bed. That's my brother's job."

"Wouldn't it be weird for you? Having to see your brother's girlfriend in that way?"

"It'll be a first for him; he's never really brought a girlfriend on tour. The rest of us have. For him to have suggested that you come with us tells me you mean more to him than he may think. I should have known once I knew you were the girl from the bar. He was really upset when you disappeared on him all those years

113

ago."

"But he didn't even know me."

"He knew enough that he wanted to be with you. By pure luck he got a second chance to see you. And this time do what he was too chicken to do then and go after you. And I'm pretty sure he'll try to convince you to stay with him in any way he can so that he doesn't lose you."

I can't hide the blush that creeps across my face. He's right on that account.

"I can tell by your reaction he already has. Just try not to hurt him too badly if you decide you don't want him," he says, as he brushes past me to drop his bag in the bedroom.

I get myself comfortable on one of the couches in the seating area to ponder what Alucard said.

Once everyone is on board, Lucius takes my hand and leads me back to the bedroom, shutting the door behind him. He starts stripping me of my clothes before removing his. Pulling the covers down from the bed, we climb in. I curl myself to his side and allow the hum of the bus and beat of his heart to lull me to sleep.

Chapter Thirteen
TONI

I'M WOKEN UP BY AN ANGRY VOICE CURSING loudly and yelling. I sit up, startled to find Lucius pulling on a pair of pants, already going to check what is happening. My only thought could be that Nicholai is on the phone with Nikki's father. I put my sweatpants and tank top back on so I can follow Lucius.

Nicholai is pacing back and forth in the bunk area with his phone to his ear. Tension rolls through his body, matching the scowl he's wearing.

"So you expect him to put up with her conning her way into his room and stalking him everywhere we go? No, if you don't tell her to leave him alone, we will be pressing charges against her." He pauses and listens. "Then maybe we need to approach another label for our next album once our contact is up, since we haven't renewed our contract yet." He pauses again. "I'm sure you'll lose more clients when word gets out that you aren't making a band happy but expect them to go through hell for your bottom line. It won't take long for it to leak out about the bullshit you expect us to put up with. And if we drop you, then people will ask questions. And we'll be honest. Unless you want us contacting another executive to tell them what's happening... You have twenty-four hours before I make the call. Goodbye."

Nicholai runs his hand through his hair before rubbing his face in frustration. The part of the call we didn't hear must not have gone as well as he hoped for.

"So, I take it he wants us to just let her do whatever she wants?" Lucius asks.

"He wants us to let it go. He says she's upset and that's why she went to you."

"Yeah, so upset that she was practically naked in my room waiting for me. She didn't expect me to have a girlfriend, which is why she contacted her father, claiming to be upset. She figured she would try crawling back and I'd welcome her in, not that it will ever happen."

Not wanting to hear more about his ex-girlfriend, I head back to the bedroom. Why I had even followed I don't know, probably to make myself suffer. I grab my tablet out of my computer bag and power it on. Thankfully, the bus has Wi-Fi and I'm able to hook into it. I check my work email and find one from both Rick and Mitch outlining what information they want for the story and that they want updates as often as possible.

I pull open my Word document and start to work on my diary entries, which is where I document most of my notes. It's an easy way to remember what I've done and what information I've gathered.

June 18th

Heading to Saskatoon today from Edmonton. This is my first day touring with the band, so I will, hopefully, get to see everything. The day started out with most everyone sleeping, seeing as the night before was a late night. PR crisis was averted, temporarily.

Saving the file before closing it out, I check my personal email. Nothing new but spam there. The bed dips, and looking up, I see Lucius looking at me as if he's worried about my reaction.

"We're about an hour and a half out and the guys want to stop for something to eat," he says. "We're making a stop in North Battleford, more selection."

"Ok," I reply, biting my lip.

"What's wrong?" he asks, picking up on my mood.

I chew on my lip as I figure out how to explain it since I know saying nothing will not make him drop it. And he deserves to know part of what's on my mind. "How long ago did you break up with Nikki?"

He frowns, obviously surprised by my question. "Three months, maybe four."

"And you said she's shown up looking for you before?"

"Yeah, she's shown up at each of my brothers' places and my parents'. She doesn't know where I'm living now."

I sigh. "So, you never figured she would pull what she did last night?"

"I figured she would have gotten the picture

when no one would tell her where I was and that I changed my number. Speaking of numbers, where's your cell phone?"

I grab my phone from beside the bed and hand it to him. I watch as he types some things into it before handing it back to me, along with his. I enter my number into his contacts list, like I assume he wants me to, before handing it back to him.

I let out a shocked screech when he grabs my ankle and pulls me toward him. Before anything else registers, his mouth is on mine, taking me in a demanding kiss. My arms wind around his neck, holding him to me, the hairs at his nape tickling my arms. Desire burns through my body as he deepens the kiss.

I whimper as he pulls away. "After we eat," he says, giving me a wicked grin. "We didn't stop before we left to grab breakfast and the guys are starving."

"Ok," I reply, as he pulls me up.

"Believe me, I want to finish what we started last night before we were interrupted."

I giggle. "So that's why you want me around, so you don't get blue balls?" I tease.

"You're the one giving them to me. I've never gotten hard just kissing someone before."

Blushing, I reply, "I've never gotten wet just from a kiss."

He curses before leading me from the room to where the guys are sitting at the front of the bus. I know I'm still blushing when I tuck my feet under me as I sit on the loveseat.

"Please tell me you are not a vegetarian," says Christoph.

I look at him and grin as I reply, "Nor am I a vegan. I don't mind salads, but I'm more of a pasta person."

"Sweet, then you won't force us to change our diets while you're with us," he says with a smirk.

"Uh, no. As long as you don't mind if I sneak chocolate on the bus, we'll be all good," I reply.

"If it's white chocolate, I'll show you a good hiding place," replies Jasper with a smirk. The smirk looks out of place compared to the usually serious, brooding, or bored expressions that he's known for. I'd probably faint if he smiled.

"You like chocolate?" I ask. His nod makes me laugh. "I'll have to remember that."

I shift my legs and lean into Lucius. He immediately wraps an arm around my shoulders, holding me to him. I figured there would be an adjustment period for the guys to get used to me being around, but it doesn't appear so. They're focused on the action movie playing on the TV. I notice that there's a DVD player on a shelf above the TV in the corner and a gaming system below.

I was so sucked in to watching the movie that I didn't notice we stopped until the driver got up from his seat. Getting up too, I head to the bedroom to grab a pair of flip flops, with Lucius close behind me to pull his boots on. Taking my hand, he leads me off the bus.

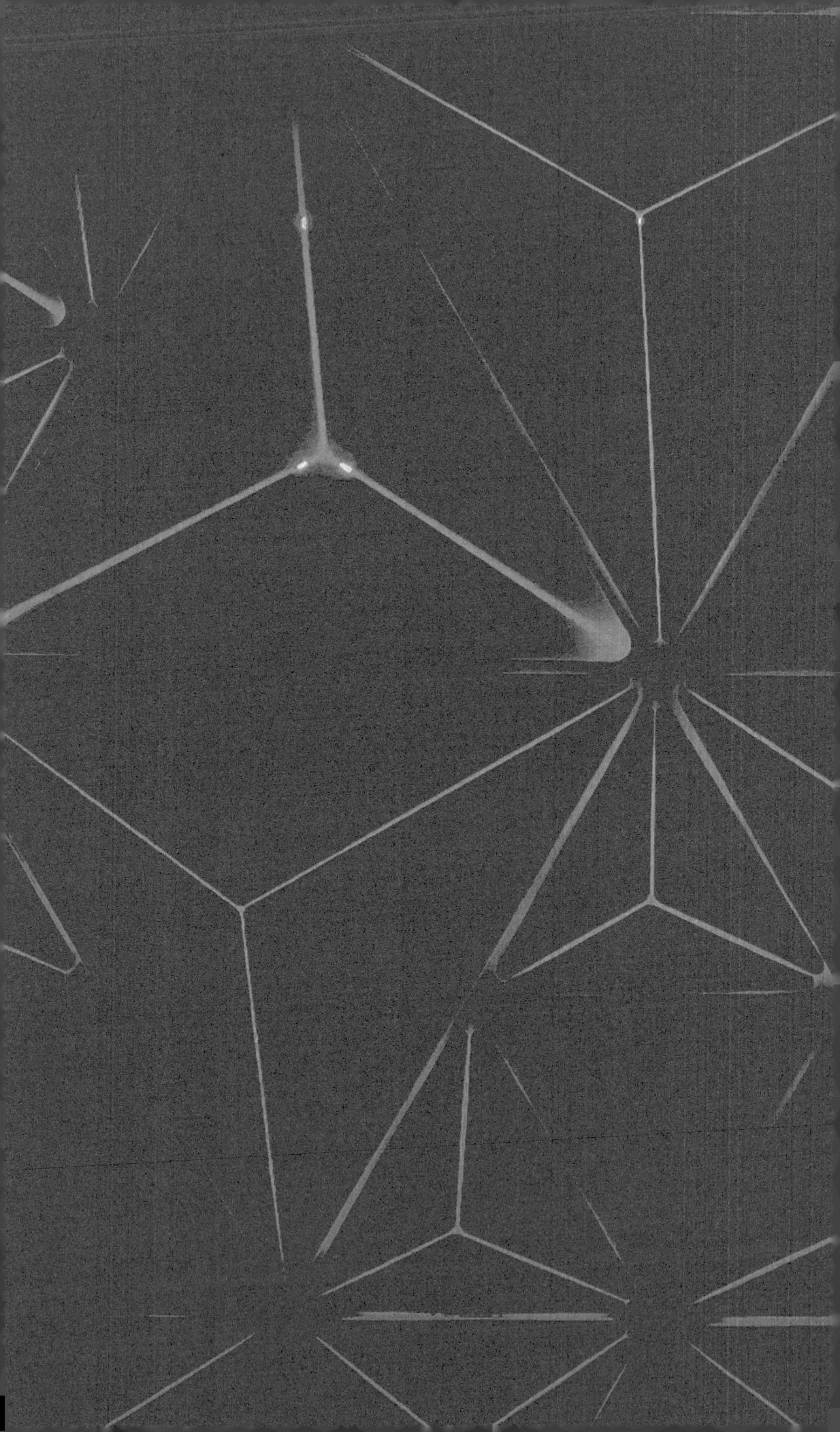

Chapter Fourteen
TONI

WE HAD PULLED INTO A WENDY'S; I WAS thankful that it wasn't a McDonald's. After having several bad experiences with McDonald's, I had decided to boycott them. It isn't busy so we're all served fairly quickly. Because of the time constraints, we have to take our food to-go and eat on the bus. I figured this would be a normal habit since they do have a tight schedule. I did learn that the roadies had left after the show last night to get to the next venue in time to start setting up. Since the guys are only needed for sound checks, they didn't need to leave so early.

As we eat, the guys fill me in on some of their childhood. Of course, they in turn ask me questions. I try not to give much away about my past, Luc being the exception to knowing how I grew up. While the guys are talking, I can't help but notice that Jasper has been fairly quiet. It makes me wonder if he really is the shy, quiet one of the group.

When we're done eating, Lucius lifts me over his shoulder and the guys laugh at my sudden shriek of surprise. Lucius carries me down the aisle of the bus to the bedroom. I'm sure my face is bright red from blushing, but it could also be the blood flowing to my head from being upside down. I grip his belt and try to push myself up.

Kicking the bedroom door closed, he slides me down his body until my feet hit the floor. Kissing, we fall into a tangle on the bed, trying to shuck our way out of our clothes as quickly as we can. The unfulfilled desire from the night before rising back to the surface with a vengeance.

He pauses long enough to grab a condom and sheath himself before thrusting into me. I gasp at the sudden entry. I grip his forearms as he stares down at me, watching me. Wrapping my arms around his neck, I tangle my fingers into his silky hair and pull him down for a kiss, needing his mouth on me to drive me farther into ecstasy.

His lips trail from my mouth to my neck, nipping at the sensitive spot just behind my ear. His thrusts are slow and deep. Not frenzied like I thought they would be, how I want them to be. I wrap my legs around his and try to leverage myself into a position that will drive him crazy. Instead, he pauses and I whimper.

My whimper must have sent him beyond his control. He begins to thrust faster and harder than before. His mouth takes mine with the same measure as his thrusts. I grip on to him, my body quivering before going tense. His kiss swallows my moans while my body tightens around his hardness as I orgasm.

When the spots behind my eyes finally clear, I find Lucius on his forearms above me, smiling. "That good?"

"I don't think I have ever come so hard," I reply, smiling up at him.

"Good," he answers. He thrusts slowly and it's only then that I realize he's still hard.

"You didn't come?" I ask.

He chuckles as he shakes his head in

response, leaning down to kiss me. It's in this moment I realize that I'm falling for this man. A man whom I'll never be able to have a proper relationship with; a man who wouldn't want a girl professing her love to him when we barely even know one another. A man who would hate me for the secret that could tear us apart. A man that, for all intents and purposes, is too good for me.

I hide my face in the crook of his neck. I can feel the buildup of my pleasure rising again as he continues to lazily thrust into me. I just hope that when I go over for the second time that he joins me, ending this moment of self-realization of how much I have fallen for him so quickly.

Chapter Fifteen
TONI

I LAY SATED IN HIS ARMS, NOT WANTING TO MOVE, but knowing we'll have to get up shortly to shower before the show. The bus had come to a stop a while ago and we're just delaying what we should be doing.

"I gotta get up for a shower, baby. I almost wish we had a larger bathroom so you can have one with me," he says with a smirk while winking.

"Yeah, like I want to be the reason the guys are yelling at us to get out of the bathroom when they need to be getting ready too," I say on an eye roll.

He kisses me quickly and gets up to have his shower. I grab his discarded shirt from earlier and pull it on, happy that it covers most of me. I pull out some clothes and look around for a towel. I open the closet door and find it packed with random stuff, but no towels. Figuring I might as well wait for Lucius to get back, I pull out my toiletry bag and makeup kit from one of my bags.

When Lucius comes in a few moments later with a towel around his waist, I pause in awe. He's a gorgeous man, even with his bad boy appearance. I hate reading the poetic crap you find in romance books when women describe their men, but for once I finally understood it. It's the way a woman feels about her man that no one else would experience the same way. It's when you find the one you are meant to be with and he's beyond reasonably attractive.

Snapping out of my stupor I ask, "Luc, where're the towels? I want to have a quick shower before everyone has to start getting ready."

"They're in the bathroom," he says, as he opens a cupboard and pulls one out for me.

Knowing that the guys need to get ready as well, I throw the towel over the glass door to the shower to at least partially hide me and quickly pull off Lucius's shirt so I can get in the shower.

I make quick work of getting washed up before wrapping the towel securely around my body. Even though Alucard attempted to make me feel comfortable around the guys, I still don't want them to see me without clothes on. It's bad enough that, aside from Luc, one of them has already seen me naked. In the bedroom I come to a halt when I find Alucard getting dressed. In addition to the tattoos, I notice the twins' body tones are slightly different, with Alucard being slightly more muscular than Lucius.

Clearing my throat to announce my presence, I say, "Don't mind me, I'm just going to quickly get dressed." Grunting his acknowledgement, Alucard gives me privacy by keeping his back to me while I quickly pull my clothes on. I grab my makeup kit and hairbrush, heading out to the front of the bus.

I know I'm blushing when I join the rest of the guys, not sure how I'll tell Lucius that I saw his brother's naked backside or his brother might have seen me naked. I start to brush the knots out of my hair quickly before fashioning it in a messy bun. Sitting at the table, I begin putting my makeup on. I don't always wear a ton, but I want to look good enough to be seen with Lucius.

Happy with my results, I pack up my stuff and bring it to the bedroom to put away. I also pull out my digital camera to bring out with me, so I can take pictures. I grab my cell phone to check for messages, but don't see anything; not that I'd expect many.

Heading back to the front of the bus, I join Lucius on the loveseat and find the guys looking at me.

"What?" I ask. "Did I mess up my makeup? Is my shirt on backwards?"

"You won't like it," starts Nicholai. "But one of our roadies has seen Nikki here. We're trying to get security to eject her, but she's threatening everyone's job."

"Let me guess, you want me to play nice?" I ask, glaring. Great. She ruined last night for us, and now she's here to stir the pot some more. Is this what I am going to have to deal with? How did Lucius put up with her when he was with her? She's nothing but a plastic, gold-digging bitch.

"We wanted to warn you so that it doesn›t

come as a complete surprise. She can be vicious, and we›d rather you be prepared for her to attack you verbally. We don't think she will actually attempt to touch you, but we'll need to make sure someone watches out for you while we're on stage."

"That's easy, I can be in front of the stage taking pictures. She won't be able to cause a scene there, with the crowd and security tonight. And maybe a good ass kicking would do her some good." It's been a while since I've been in a fight, not that I enjoy it, but I had to learn to protect myself at one point.

"Baby," Lucius says, "if you touch her, she'll go after you with cops and a lawsuit. I don't want that to happen. We don't know why she showed up again other than to try to cause trouble."

"We don't need you getting into trouble because she's trying to cause a problem. By bringing you with us we've taken on the responsibility to ensure your safety and keep you out of trouble," Alucard interjects.

"I'll behave," I agree on an eye roll. "Last thing I want would be to have anything come back on you guys. Or even my own bosses."

Before we can say anything else, someone comes up the stairs of the bus. He has reddish hair that sticks out in all directions from under his hat and pale green eyes that are shining with excitement. He's wearing a black Twisted Tragic crew shirt. "They're ready for you," he says, before disappearing.

Lucius takes my hand and pulls me up and we all head from the bus to the arena. With my camera around my neck, I figure it will be a good time to take some pictures while they do their sound checks. It will also give me a chance to observe them and write about this.

A couple of security guards escort us from the private entrance we came in, down to the back of the makeshift stage. Lucius points to a spot that will take me around to the front of the stage and kisses me before heading up to take his place. I make my way around the side to the front and find I have a five foot space to work with between the stage and the barrier. I watch as the guys take their places and try to find the best vantage points for getting pictures before I start taking them.

"Oh look, if it isn't the groupie whore," an irritating voice says. I'd rather listen to nails on chalkboard than her.

Knowing that it's Nikki, I ignore her and continue taking pictures. I know the guys are watching despite needing to focus on rehearsal and won't be happy if I say or do anything. I really want to give her a piece of my mind and tell her to fuck off and leave Lucius alone. And to admit that she lied about being pregnant since she surely doesn't look it. She's as skinny as a twig.

"You do know that he'll eventually get bored of a mousy girl like you and toss you aside."

I clench my teeth to keep from whipping around and telling her what a bitch she really is. I pull out my phone and put it on record, hoping to catch what she is saying, to use against her, something I should have done after the first comment.

Cat got your tongue, whore? Or maybe you were sucking too much cock that your jaw hurts and you can't move it."

I close my eyes and take a deep breath to steady my emotions. She's trying to get a rise out of me, and if I can just stay calm she won't get the satisfaction she is looking for. I need to keep the whirlwind of emotions I'm feeling hidden so that not only she can't see it, but the guys can't either. They don't need to know the pain I feel at her words.

"You do know he's only using you to make me jealous, right? He'll take me back and leave you to be the pathetic little slut he used. He doesn't like girls who are easy, he likes the challenge some women know how to give him; a woman like me."

I take another deep, calming breath. I start to count backward from ten. I need to calm my anger before I let her have it.

"Why he picked you to be the one to try to make me jealous, I have no clue; you're not even pretty. You're just a fugly little whore. And God knows what you might have. I'd have to make him get tested so that I don't catch whatever it is that you have."

A loud distorted sound comes over the speakers and Alucard is approaching the front of the stage with Lucius right behind him. Both wearing pissed off expressions. They must have seen mine and know that something is about to go down. They're saving me from unleashing my fury on the pathetic bitch.

"Nikki, get the fuck out of here," says Alucard angrily.

"Aww, big brother has to fight your battles for you, Luc?," she says.

"Nikki, we're done. You have no business being here," Lucius says. I can tell he's pissed. Once again I'm glad it's not at me. Both of them look scary, like grizzly bears being woken from hibernation.

Lucius waves a security guard over and tells him to remove Nikki and to ensure that she doesn't get back in tonight or any other night.

As the guard takes Nikki by the arm and starts to lead the way out she starts screaming threats.

I turn off the recording I was making and turn to face the guys. "If she gets in again, I'm not going to put up with the verbal abuse. I will knock her on her ass," I fume. "If you want her dad to believe you're serious about keeping her away, you can play the recording I just took of what she's saying. I don't know how clear it is with the music playing, but it's got to be something that can help get rid of her." I know my voice is betraying my fury at the horrid woman.

Lucius hands his guitar to his brother and hops off the stage, pulling me into his arms. "She's gone now. It's ok, baby."

I pull back, "No, it's not ok. She can't keep stalking you. She can't keep treating people like crap. And she has no right to be calling people sluts or whores when she doesn't even know them. She's delusional if she thinks you would even consider taking her back. I was ready to turn around and deck her regardless of the consequences."

Pulling away, I turn around and storm off, completely and utterly pissed. What pisses me off even more are the tears that escape because of how angry I am. I know I'll have to touch up my makeup, so I make my way back to the bus. A few of the things she said struck a nerve because I have thought them too; that he will leave me and that he deserves better. Especially someone who won't hide a terrible secret from him like I am.

When I get to the bus, I head to the bedroom to get my stuff so I can clean my face off and reapply my makeup. I tune everything out as I get myself ready, knowing that I'll need to be composed when I face the guys. They don't need to know how badly Nikki upset me, nor do they need to know my own self-conscious thoughts of inadequacy. Lucius doesn't need to know how insecure I feel about myself, nor how worried I am that what we have won't last.

Once my makeup is fixed, I grab my notebook and head to the kitchen table to have someplace to sit with it. Turning it on, I start to upload the few pictures I took so I can look through them. I got some really good shots of them doing their soundcheck, for the short time I was there. I start writing a little bit in my daily journal in hopes to continue with my distraction.

I'm shocked to see Jasper climb the stairs of the bus alone. I figured the guys would be with him. I give him a timid smile, not sure of what to say to him and scared of what might come out if I do talk to him. I'm embarrassed because I don't know how to talk to him. It's that awkward feeling that you get when you don't know how to approach a subject with someone, so you sit in silence instead.

"I'm sorry you had to put up with Nikki," he says, sounding remorseful as he runs a hand through the longer hair at the top of his head. It's something that I've noticed he does a lot, almost like it's a nervous habit. A habit that leaves his hair looking sexy as hell, not that I'm interested in him that way.

"You have nothing to be sorry about, Jasper. It isn't any of your fault that she's a total bitch and showed up. But I did get some good pictures while I was there. Want to see?" I ask to change the subject. I really don't want to get worked up again after finally calming myself down.

His face changes into a smile from the serious look he had before. Damn, he's gorgeous. I move over so that Jasper can sit next to me to see the pictures as I flip through them. I almost wonder if I can talk to him now or if we'll get interrupted. But how the hell do I bring up the subject?

"We should post some of these on social media to hype people up for the show tonight," he says, as he checks out the pictures.

"We can do that. Next time, I think I want to try to get some from maybe the front of the stage, where I can try to move around and get better shots. You know, right on the stage."

Jasper gets up and goes to his bunk, returning with a tablet. "Let's get you added to our social media accounts so I can make you an admin."

Blushing, I say, "I'm already on the group's Facebook page and individual pages. I also follow on Twitter and Instagram."

I blush even more when Jasper chuckles. "Makes it easier for me to make you an admin so you can post stuff. Just make sure nothing too personal ends up on them. We usually have no problems with our individual accounts, but occasionally we may want you to upload some of these to them for us. Plus, our personal accounts are left so no one can find us on them; any searches lead to our public pages. So we'll each have to add you as friends to those accounts. Only our close friends and family can see anything on those. I'm sure Lucius will want to make it known he's off the market again by posting a picture of the two of you together."

"Yeah, that's not happening on any of the public pages. I don't need people randomly coming up to me on the street," I reply. I honestly don't want our relationship to be public knowledge. It's not that I want him to hide me from the public, I just want our relationship to be as private as possible rather than open for the world to see and judge.

Jasper makes quick work of getting me added to almost everything and refers me as a friend to the rest of the guys to add me to their private accounts. I'm shocked when Lucius adds me and then an "In a relationship" status request pops up, one asking me to confirm.

A video call shows up on Jasper's tablet which he answers. He introduces me to his sister, Jade, who I find out is actually his twin. While he talks to her briefly, I start to upload a couple pictures to the different accounts. I try to give him privacy by ignoring him.

"Hey, Jade," a familiar deep voice says behind me. Looking up with a smile, I find Lucius leaning down to see Jade before leaning over to kiss me. If the kiss was meant to make me want him right now, then it worked. I kiss him back before he pulls away. He has a mischievous grin on his face.

"What are you up to?" I ask cautiously, afraid of what he might say. If it's one thing I hate it is a surprise.

"Just wait and see," he says, still grinning as he taps away at his phone.

My computer pings and I look. My jaw drops and my face goes bright red. He posted and tagged me in a picture he snuck of us kissing just now. My family will see this and they have no idea that I'm even dating anyone.

"Oh my God. Everyone's going to see that and no one knows I'm even in a relationship. It's not even like we've been together long." Glaring at him, I hiss, "I was going to wait until I told my family and we knew what was going on between us before I announced anything."

I pull out my cell phone and send a group text to my family.

Me: Sorry about the social media announcement. My new boyfriend didn't want to wait till I could tell you first before announcing that we're together. And I apologize for anything he posts that may not be the most appropriate content.

Thankfully, Jasper moved out of the way so that Lucius could sit next to me and I don't have to raise my voice for everyone to hear. The last thing I want is to embarrass myself by having a fight in front of everyone. I know eventually we'll fight in front of the guys, but I didn't figure it would be so soon.

"Hey, it was just meant to be playful," he says softly. He wraps an arm around me and pulls me into his side, kissing the top of my head. "I didn't think you would get upset about it."

"Playful is one thing. Announcing to the world we're together is another. We don't even know what it is that we have, or where we're going with it. I haven't even had a chance to tell my family, which now I just had to send them a text so they don't freak out. They may freak out anyway, especially my adopted brother."

"We can delete it if it's that much of a bother to you," he says with concern and a touch of hurt in his voice.

I let out a sigh. "No, it's fine. It'll eventually get out. I'd have just liked to have had the chance to tell them first." I snuggle into his side, oblivious to anything else but him. And to hide from my obvious freak out.

His chest shakes with a silent chuckle against my cheek. Pulling away from him, I return my attention to my notebook. I find several new notifications and my face turns beet red with embarrassment at comments to the picture and relationship status. Of course, the guys had to make teasing comments. Also, a friend request from Jaded Hart, and I see that she's friends with all the guys. I think to myself this must be Jasper's sister.

My stomach lets out a betraying growl. We had a late breakfast, but skipped lunch, and I'm actually hungry. I may have to see if we can stock up on some snacks and maybe a few meal replacement shakes if we're going to be eating at odd times.

"We've got time before the show actually starts, want to go out and get something to eat?" Lucius asks.

"Is it safe to even go out in public?" I ask, knowing that if he's recognized he may get mobbed by fans. Something I really wasn't looking forward to happening.

"We either go out to eat or we order in and have to share with the rest of the guys."

"Why don't we see if we can order in, and when we get to a bigger city you can take me out. Less chance of getting recognized," I answer with a smirk.

Lucius turns to Nicholai, "Hey, Nic, can you order in some food?"

"Sure."

He then takes my hand and pulls me from the table back toward the bedroom, wanting to have some time alone with me before we spend the evening with everyone else.

Chapter Sixteen
TONI

DURING THE SHOW I MOVE AROUND THE FRONT of the stage taking pictures. I've made sure to get some shots of the crowd, figuring it would be a good idea for fans to tag themselves for being at the show. I'm going to leave that decision up to the guys. I even managed to get a couple of really good shots of Jasper and Christoph hiding in the back.

As the show ends, I make my way toward the side of the stage to get back in behind. Sadly, I'm detained by one of the local security guys who is refusing to let me get by. When he refuses to even try to verify that I should be allowed backstage, I decide to send a text to Lucius, hoping he has his phone with him.

The security guard is my height of five foot six, and extremely stocky. Looking at his name tag, I address this cocky asshole, "Listen, Sean. I'm with the band. I'm part of their Social Media team. I don't have a pass made yet, but they will verify I'm allowed past."

"I don't care who you are, lady. No pass. No access," he says sternly.

"I don't think you heard me. I'm with the band. Hell, anyone can tell you that not only am I part of their team, but I am also dating Lucius Black," I reply. I can hear the frustration in my voice. "How about you speak to one of your buddies backstage to verify. Tell them to talk to any one of the guys in the band and they will vouch for me."

"Listen up, chick. I've heard all sorts of excuses from girls trying to get backstage. You don't have a pass, so I'm not going to let you through. Now back off."

One of the stage hands overhears my argument with the security personnel and comes to my rescue, telling him that I was ok to pass, that I really was with the band and hadn't had a chance to have my ID card made yet. The security guard, Sean, tells him that if I don't have the proper credentials, I am not getting past that point.

Daniel, as it turned out, is their head engineer. He managed to get someone to go look for one of the guys so I could get past the moron barring my way. I was hoping this would not be a problem next time, because if it was, it's not going to be fun always having to wait for someone to come get me. I suppose I should be somewhat thankful that security is so tight. It means fewer random women can get backstage.

I was glad that Christoph came to rescue me. I thanked Daniel for his help and followed Christoph backstage. There are clusters of people milling around, most having booze in hand. Christoph points me in the direction of Lucius and then heads off in another direction.

When I step through the doorway into the dressing room, I find it packed with people. I hate small spaces, there's no way I'm going to brave the room just to find him. I figure it will be best to head to the bus and start to upload some of the shots I took. I was just about to turn when someone shifts and I see him standing near the back of the room. He looks up and sees me in that moment and pushes away from whoever he is talking to, making his way to me with a sexy as hell grin on his handsome face.

"Hey, baby," he says, before giving me a quick kiss.

"Hey," I reply back, grinning.

"I have someone I want you to meet." His tone is excited, even though I know he's probably tired from performing.

Taking my hand, he leads me back to who he was speaking with, grabbing a beer for us both as we go past a bucket overflowing with bottles. Alucard is with whoever else Luc was speaking to. When we're close enough, I notice a resemblance between the stranger and the brothers and quickly realize it's another sibling.

Clasping his hand over the man's shoulder, Luc says, "Damien, I want you to meet Toni. Toni, this is one of my brothers, Damien."

"Hi," he says, as he shakes my hand.

"Hello," I reply politely, almost shyly.

Damien looks a lot like his younger brothers except he's shorter. Apparently, he was in the area and decided to come see his brothers before they left.

Damien asks me a fair number of questions

since he noticed his brothers' social media status updates and recognizes me from the picture posted earlier. I try not to reveal too much about myself because there's so much that I don't want the general public to know about me; mostly about my upbringing. Damien seems to be fairly laid back, even if his job requires a lot of travel like mine. He's vague about what he does, which I'd expect since he doesn't know me from a hole in the ground and the fact that I'm being just as vague. Depending on how things go with Lucius, eventually he will probably open up to me more, and likely I'll open up to him too.

After a while, Lucius excuses us and gives his brother a hug before leading us out of the dressing room. I find myself laughing because of the pace he's set, and I'm struggling to keep up due to the difference in our height. Careful of my camera, he throws me over his shoulder, with me letting out a shriek, and he carries me back to the bus, fans going nuts as we pass by them. I can't help but laugh at his behaviour and knowing his sweat-covered clothes are going to make mine damp.

He places me on the bottom step of the bus so I can make my way up without him hurting me. He puts my camera down on the table with my notebook and keeps pushing me toward the back of the bus. Before we even get to the room he's kissing me hungrily, lifting me so that I can wrap my legs around his waist.

Reluctantly pulling away, I say, "Go have a shower, I still have work to do. We have plenty of time later to continue this."

With a sigh, he lowers me down, even though I know he doesn't want to wait. I move to go past him when we hear a scream of pleasure along with a few grunts and moans come from the bedroom area. I glance at the door and back at Lucius. He shrugs. "Probably Christoph or Nicholai with some chick. Good thing we didn't interrupt them."

"Yeah, that would have been awkward," I reply. Especially since I know I wouldn't want to be walked in on. I'm just glad I'm not as vocal as whoever the chick is, or at least Luc doesn't let me be. I head toward the kitchenette to get started on sorting through the pictures I took tonight and doing a quick write-up while my hotter than sin boyfriend showers. To focus, I throw on my playlist and headphones. My fingers fly across the keyboard as I type up some info on today's events, leaving out the PR nightmare that is his ex.

When I get to the photos, I start to edit some of them to make them a little better. I'm so lost in what I'm doing I nearly jump when the seat shifts next to me on the bench. Pulling off one side of my headphones as I turn, I notice Jasper sitting next to me. I show him some of the pictures I took and he suggests a few to post. I show him the crowd shot and he likes the idea of posting it so fans can tag themselves to show they were there. I log in to Facebook and start uploading a few of them into the group page and then adding ones of each of them to their individual pages.

While I'm logged in, I check my own notifications to see I was tagged in a photo and can't help but laugh. Lucius posted a picture of me with my headphones on and typing. You can tell I'm focused on what I'm doing. He captioned it as *"My girl hard at work when we should be having fun!"*

Moving on to the other social media sites, I start posting other pictures and have Jasper help caption them so that it will sound like their words. Once I get an idea of how they talk and post, I'll be able to do it on my own. When I get to Lucius's pages I notice that he's already updated them himself and announced our relationship without adding pictures. Knowing he'll want to post pictures of us, I'll have to figure out a way to get some good ones that I'd approve of.

Finally finished with everything, I shut down my computer. Turning to Jasper beside me, I say, "I'm going to need to stop to get another external drive, mine won't have enough space to hold all the pictures I'll be taking while I'm with you, and I don't like deleting stuff."

"We'll be in Winnipeg all day tomorrow, so we'll get to go out for a while. You can stop to get one then," he replies.

"So, what happens when you have short travel distances? Do you get a hotel when you're there or just stay on the bus?" I ask. It's something I'm actually curious about, but never really thought to ask.

"Depends on when we get in and if it's worth it. Most times we just park and stay on the bus. Only time we really get hotels is if we plan to stay for a couple of days. I think Toronto we're staying for a couple of nights before moving on, so we'll have a hotel there."

"Does it ever get weird being on the bus all the time?" I ask.

"Sometimes we miss having space, but we've got lots to keep us entertained. We have video games, movies, usually we have beer, and sometimes we have board games. It just depends on what we're in the mood for. I'm usually online most of the time trying to keep up with the social media, so having you here will help and make things go a bit quicker. When we're somewhere early enough in the day we try to escape and go out for a while."

"You guys must have to sacrifice a lot." I can hear the awe in my voice as I speak.

"Not really. It's something we love to do. The only hard thing is being away from family for extended periods of time. It's why I Skype with my sister when I can. And it can make relationships hard. Only having little bits of time with someone, we try to make it work when it's serious to bring them with us for a bit or fly them in for a weekend when we're able to. But for the most part it's phone calls and video chats."

"So, who all is single in the group?" I ask, more so to start gathering information about them for the article my bosses want.

"Let's just say Lucius is the only lucky bastard right now," he says with a smirk.

Confused I ask, "None of you have girlfriends right now?"

"Nope. But if my sister had her way, Christoph wouldn't be single. She thinks she's not being obvious about her feelings, but she is. I've known she's liked him for a while now. But he wouldn't date her because of me."

"He's scared you would go all big brother?" I ask teasingly. He grins, which transforms his face. He really is a beautiful man.

"No, he respects me enough to know that dating my sister would only cause a rift between us if things went wrong. My sister is naive when it comes to what it would take to be with one of us. It's going to be hard for you once you have to go back to work. I think that's why Luc suggested you help me out, so that he can be selfish and keep you with him. Not that I mind, but eventually, you will need space from being around guys all the time and will want to have girl time."

I laugh. "The only girl time I spend is with Keri. I don't have any girlfriends except for her. I'm more of a loner than anything. With my work I can be gone for long periods at a time, so it works for me. There's times when I've been gone for a few weeks to come home for a couple of days only to turn around and leave again for a few more weeks."

"Just to warn you, my sister will eventually be hassling you about hanging out and getting gossip. She can drive some people nuts, so don't be afraid to tell her no. If she's that much of a pain in the ass you can always let me know and I can deal with her."

"I can handle my own battles. I'm not afraid to speak my mind. I almost lost it earlier with that bitch, and that was tough not to."

"Anyway, you might want to go see your man. Looks like he's already gone to bed. Pansy needs his beauty rest."

I giggle. "Oh my God. You did not just call him that."

"Fuck, that's tame compared to the insults we give each other. I'm just being nice since you're his woman."

I giggle more. "Ok, I'll see you later," I say, as I get up and head to the bedroom.

I find Lucius laying on the bed in nothing but a pair of boxers, the view making me smile. Pulling on a tank top and shorts, I climb on the bed with him.

"So, you really want to be posting pictures of us together and announcing to the world that you belong to me and I to you?" Luc nods his head. "I have a compromise. I get to approve any photos before you post them; no random posting like you did earlier." I curl myself up next to him, laying my head on his chest. Taking my phone, I try to find a flattering angle before snapping the picture. Showing it to him I say, "This is something I would approve of."

I let him watch me as I post it to Facebook and tag him in it. Then I go to the other social media sites, posting and tagging him. I then set my phone down and kiss him. He pulls me tighter to him as he deepens the kiss, our legs becoming tangled.

A knock on the door prevents us from going any farther. I let out a sigh while Lucius groans before calling out to whoever is there to go away.

We aren't so lucky. Damien and Alucard come in, ignoring the request to leave us alone. I attempt to pull away, but Lucius holds me in place. My cheeks heat with embarrassment; he's using me as a shield to hide his erection from his brothers. I can only hope my ass cheeks aren't showing out of the bottom of my shorts.

"Do you mind?" Lucius growls. "We're kind of in the middle of something."

I hide my face in his chest, knowing I'm blushing even more. He's basically telling his brothers that we were about to have sex. Not that we can really hide it from the guys, but we can be as discreet as possible.

"Luc, this is serious," Damien says, his tone sounding both irritated and stern. "Nikki called Mom and Dad. Told them a ton of shit that we don't believe but could potentially cause problems."

Lucius's body turns rigid. I pull away. "I'll give you guys space to talk."

Alucard looks at me. "This involves you too. You might want to stay to hear this."

Damien sighs. "Nikki told Mom and Dad that you were controlling and abusive to her. Let's just say she went into great detail about instances that she was accusing you of. Not only that, but she's also told them that you're a drug addict and an alcoholic. She also said that Toni is a low life call girl you hired to try to make her jealous, to try to get her back. That's what threw us because she's been the one trying to get you back."

"Fuck! I've never fucking hit a woman in my life! Mom would have our balls if any of us did. And controlling? She fucking dragged me to all these stupid events I never wanted to go to, just so she could show off. Maybe occasionally I was controlling in the bedroom, but that's as far as it went," he replies angrily. "She doesn't fucking know anything about Toni."

"And I'm sure I would know if our brother was a drug addict or an alcoholic. We all enjoy a drink or two after a show to unwind, but Luc rarely drinks more than one. Fuck, he's like the old man of the group, always in bed well before the rest of us," Alucard says, shaking his head.

I'm so pissed I see red and my eyes fill with tears. Blinking them away, I glare at the wall. "If I'm a call girl, why the fuck am I busting my ass as a research assistant for a magazine? I'm sorry, but I'm done with this bitch. Next time I see her I'm going to kick her ass. To hell if I end up in jail and need to be bailed out. After the verbal assault I had to deal with today, I'm not putting up with that shit."

"What the fuck was she saying?" Lucius asked.

I grab my cell phone and play what I recorded. You can clearly hear what Nikki said over the music. "And this is just the end of it before you kicked her out of the arena."

Lucius grabs my phone and heads out of the room. We can hear muffled shouting and I'm almost terrified to find out what's being said. Most likely a heated conversation trying to deal with the Nikki situation. The woman is becoming a thorn in our sides, affecting everyone and not just mine and Lucius's relationship.

It feels like an eternity before Lucius returns to the room. Damien and Alucard are speaking quietly while I lose myself in thought. Most girlfriends wouldn't put up with the BS from an ex trying to make life miserable. The three previous relationships I've had were never really serious, so this is new territory for me. With our relationship being so new, I have no idea how serious we are or will be. This could just be him having fun and I'm the rebound girl after Nikki.

When Lucius returns to us, he has a smug look. "She won't be a problem anymore. If she does try to contact anyone in the family, Mr. Goldburg won't be happy with her and won't care what we choose to do. He'll support any decision we make when it comes to her."

Damien relaxes. It's obvious that she's being a pain in the ass to the family, and the news pleases him. Alucard has an expression of doubt on his face, and I was going to side with him because I don't think anything is going to stop her from tormenting the family or us. I can only hope that her dad stays true to his word with helping to keep his daughter away from us.

Before Damien leaves, he turns to me. "Don't be breaking my baby brother's heart. He's been through enough as it is." From the tone of his voice I can tell he cares about his brother, even if the words don't match the tone.

Before I can reply, he turns and leaves the room. I'm sure I have a stunned expression on my face. That's two Black brothers telling me not to break Lucius's heart, but no one is considering him breaking mine. Then again, neither of them know about the secret I'm keeping that could end things. Alucard leaves with his brother, no doubt to see him off since we're probably leaving soon.

My excitement effectively ruined, I crawl under the covers in hopes to sleep, or maybe just sit and talk with Lucius since we're supposed to get to know one another better. Lucius pulls me against him as I curl into him.

"What got you into music?" I ask, trying to distract both of us. Mostly because my mood has been ruined by his brothers' visit.

"Our parents tried to get us into activities when we were kids to keep us out of trouble.

Five boys could be a handful, especially us. So, we were required to do one sport and one educational activity. We played a variety of sports, practiced martial arts, and it wasn't until we hit sixth grade that Alucard and I got into music and started learning different instruments. We both fell in love with guitar and kept up with it; we were naturally good," he replies.

"Who's your favourite brother?"

His chest rumbles with laughter. "Aside from Alucard I'd have to say I'm closest to our eldest brother, Marius. He was always stopping the others from picking on me, especially Alucard. I spent more time with him than I did with my other brothers. Alucard was always the first to do anything. Marius would spend time with me trying to help me get caught up to Alucard. Alucard and I were bonded, and for the longest time our parents couldn't separate us. We had to sleep in the same bed, and if they didn't let us we'd have a meltdown. I shared a room with my brother until we moved out."

"Did you and Alucard ever pretend to be the other growing up?"

"When we were really young and no one could tell us apart we did. As we got older, we stopped because our personalities were so different. Alucard was all about being popular and I was all about making good grades. He's always been more of a partier than I am."

"What are your parents like?"

"For having raised five boys, they're pretty laid back. They both have awesome jobs, which is how they could afford to have all of us. Alucard and I weren't planned. Our parents had been surprised when we came along; they had only planned on having our older brothers. Mom is always cooking and baking. When she knows we're home, she either makes us go over for dinner or actually delivers dinner to us. Our dad, let's just say was the one who was the sports fan pushing us into playing. He was disappointed that none of us loved sports as much as he wanted us to; he wanted a claim to fame. Alexander was pretty close to going pro for hockey, though, before he had an accident that broke his leg. He lost his scholarship and any pro chances. It was a hard blow for not only Alexander, but for my dad."

"I wish I had grown up with parents who cared," I said sadly.

"Your mom was that bad?"

"My childhood was horrible. I was picked on by the kids I envied, all because she didn't care enough about me. How can you have a kid and not try to take care of them? I never want to subject kids to that."

Lucius tips my head up to meet his gaze. "I bet you would make an awesome mother because I know you would treat your kids the way you wanted to be treated as a kid."

"You sound so sure of that. Thankfully, I'm on birth control so I don't have to worry about getting pregnant. Between that and condoms, I think I'm covered. Besides, I'm too young to be thinking about starting a family, and we don't know what this is yet."

"I know where I want this to be going right now," he says huskily, as he leans his head toward mine and kisses me.

Chapter Seventeen
TONI

IHAD WISHED LUCIUS ADMITTED WHERE HE wanted to see us going rather than seducing me. I wanted validation that he is falling for me just as much as I am falling for him. But I promised myself I wouldn't let my insecurities show. Especially lying in his arms in the afterglow of making love.

I can tell he's sleeping by the steady rise and fall of his chest where my head rests. I can't shut my mind down, so I opt to slip from his arms and pull on a pair of shorts and a hoodie to head out to the front of the bus. It's quiet so I know most of the guys are sleeping or at least trying to. I power on my notebook, slip on my headphones, and lose myself in my work by writing down the information that I managed to get today.

I startle when I feel someone sit next to me on the bench of the table; I wasn't expecting anyone else to be awake. Pulling off my headphones, I turn to Alucard who took the seat next to me. "Can't sleep?" he asks quietly.

"No, it's normal for me to have trouble sleeping," I answer. I had to train myself to run on little sleep as a child; I never knew when or if anything would happen to me. "I usually only sleep for a few hours a night, until the weekend when I really crash."

"Let's hope maybe you get used to sleeping when you can; some of our days can be a little crazy."

I suppress a giggle. "I'm pretty sure it's crazy most days for all of you."

"Listen. I want to apologize about both me and Damien telling you to be careful not to hurt our brother. We obviously don't want him to get hurt, and we don't want to see him go through what he did with his ex-girlfriends. I know you're different for him, he's different. He's happier than he's been in a while."

"Don't worry about it, Alucard. Sure, at first, hearing you say it rubbed me the wrong way. But it shows you care about your brother enough to want to see him happy. If I were closer to my brother and sister, I'd probably say the same things to their boyfriends or girlfriends. If it means anything, I don't want to hurt him, nor do I want to get hurt."

"Toni, if Luc hurts you it won't be on purpose. It would probably be from an out of context situation that happens. Anyway, I thought I'd apologize since Luc isn't around to hear it." The smirk he wears makes me wonder if he ever actually apologizes in front of anyone.

I watch as he gets up and heads back toward the bunks. I power off my notebook and go to bed, hoping I can get some sleep, knowing that sometime tomorrow we'll be in Winnipeg with a rush to set up for the show.

I strip down and slip into bed hoping to not wake Lucius. He growls as he pulls me into his arms and I can't help but let out a giggle. "I didn't mean to wake you," I say quietly.

His mouth takes mine in a possessive kiss, one that leaves me breathless and wanting more. I press my body to his in a silent demand, hoping he understands what I want.

I'm gasping for breath when he pulls away. Reaching blindly beside the bed he comes back with a condom. Rising up, he easily flips me to my stomach and pulls my hips back. Before I can register anything, I hear the telltale sound of the wrapper being torn open. I let out a silent scream when he thrusts into me from behind, burying himself to the hilt. I'm stretched around him, feeling him all the way to my womb.

He pauses, as if trying to compose himself, and I groan. I don't know why, but I want him to take me hard and fast. I try to push back against him, but there's no give. I rock forward only for him to grip my hips to keep me still.

"Baby, don't. I'm two seconds away from coming with how tight you feel." His voice sounds strained.

After a few moments, he begins to move in fast, measured thrusts. Though it's not as hard as I want it, he's still hitting places in me that stir my pleasure. I moan into the mattress, trying to stay quiet so we don't wake the others. Even though they know we are bound to be having sex at points during the trip, they don't need to know exactly when.

My toes curl as my body tenses. My release is so close I can feel myself gripping him. As I slip over the edge, I can feel him swell within my tightening muscles. I know I'll be tender with how deep he is as he comes with me.

Collapsing on me, he attempts to keep some of his weight off me by using his forearms to support himself. I can feel his warm panting on my neck as he catches his breath. Moments later, he slides himself from me to discard the condom before pulling me back into his arms.

Resting my head on his shoulder, I drift to sleep with a satisfied smile on my face.

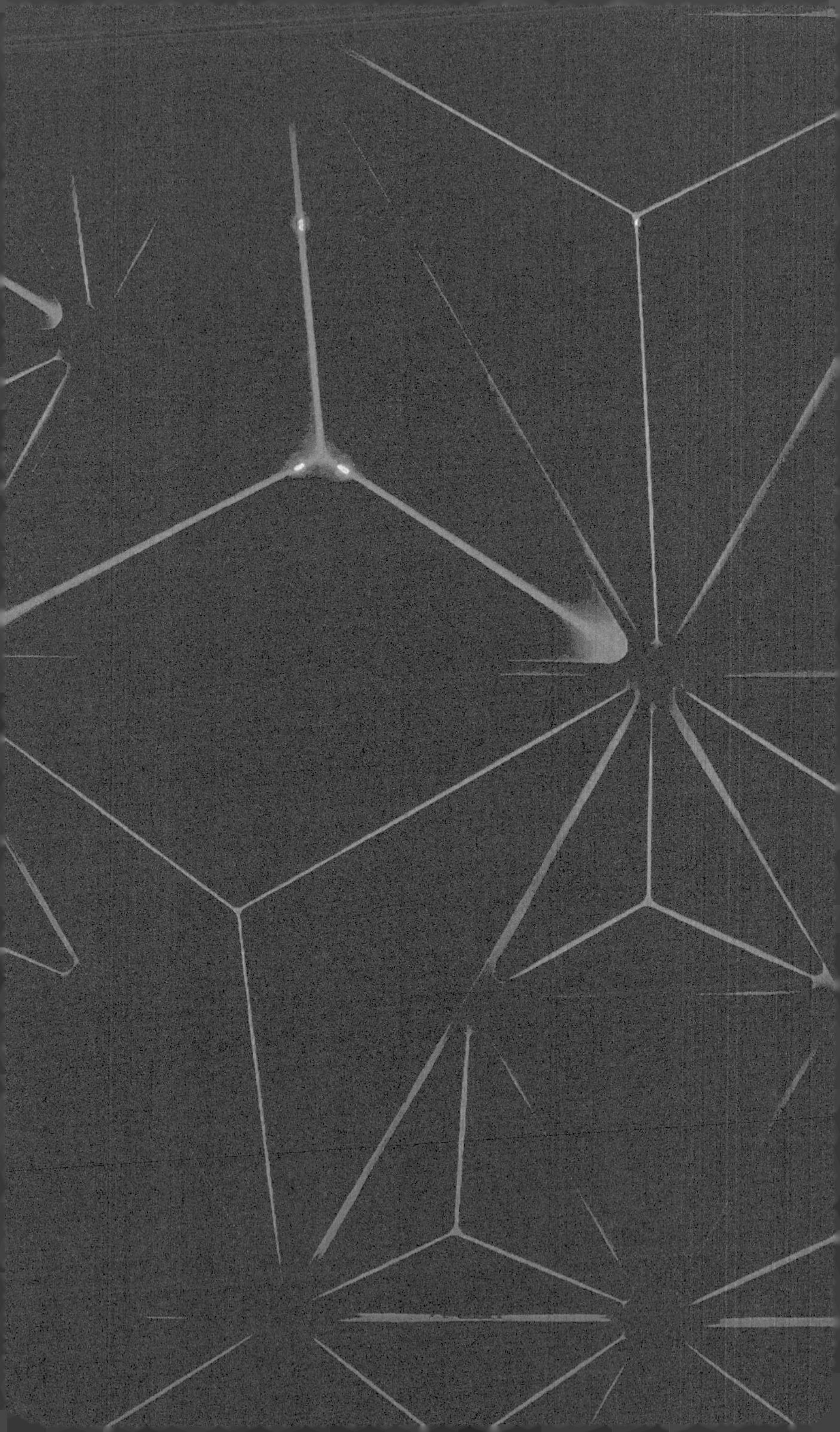

Chapter Eighteen
TONI

When I wake, muted light is filtering in from the darkened windows. It takes me a moment to realize I'm on the bus and not in my room. I reach for my phone to check what time it is. I gasp when I realize it's noon. I've never slept this long before.

Getting up, I toss on a pair of sweats and a baggy sweatshirt before I head out to the front of the bus. I blush when I realize I'm the last one up and that the guys are all sitting around the TV playing games while Jasper sits in front of his computer at the table.

Standing there watching them interact with each other, I can't help but smile. They constantly rib one another, truly acting like a family. Jasper is sitting fairly quietly, only adding an insult here and there. It's hard to believe that I'll be spending a month with them and getting to know them better.

"Do we have anything to snack on?" I ask, knowing my body is wanting food.

"Check the cupboards," replies Christoph. "There might be something in there. Usually the bus is stocked for us before we leave."

As I root through the cupboards I'm surprised to find that there is actual food on board. Although, most of it is junk food. I find a box of cereal, amused that they would have any. I check the fridge and find milk. I bring my bowl of cereal and sit across from Jasper to eat. As I sit and eat, I watch the boys play their game, noticing how competitive they are. They get louder and I wonder if they tried to keep their volume down while I was asleep.

"Wanna come distract your man, Toni?" Nicholai asks. "He's kicking our asses."

I laugh. "Uh, I don't want to piss him off."

"Good call," Jasper replies with a smirk. "He gets mad if he's winning and someone distracts him so that he loses. They're all a bunch of poor losers."

"Fuck you, Jasper," Christoph says.

I can't help but laugh. "I'm sure Jasper doesn't swing your way, Christoph."

Everyone bursts out laughing except Christoph, who glares at me, making me laugh even harder than I already am. I can't help it, it's like he's sulking, even though everyone is just playing around. But this is the first I'm seeing their normal group dynamic, considering the vast majority of my travel time so far has been spent in the bedroom with my sexy as sin boyfriend. Wow. It felt weird but so right to call Lucius my boyfriend.

When I'm done eating, I clean up what I used and take a seat on the couch between Christoph and Nicholai so I can watch the guys play. Soon enough, I'm telling them what to do in order to try to help them beat Lucius. But even with my help they still lose.

They pack away the controllers, knowing they will have to start getting ready for sound checks soon. I head back to the bedroom to get dressed in actual clothes rather than the sweats I have on. I pull out a pair of jeans and root through my bag for a decent shirt; I want to look nice for the guys.

I find a shirt that will be comfortable for taking pictures while still being dressy enough to look good, and I smile to myself. It's the first time I've wanted to dress nice for someone else. Even for past boyfriends I never really tried or thought about what I wore. But then again, Lucius isn't just any other man. He's a man many people drool over, and his female fans have expectations of the type of woman he should be with.

I quickly change, knowing the guys will want to get in and start getting ready. Once I'm dressed, I grab my makeup bag and head to the front of the bus.

Sitting across from Jasper again, I begin the task of getting my makeup on. I can see Jasper shake his head out of the corner of my eye. Men never understand why a girl wears so much stuff in order to look pretty, when they just toss on whatever without a care. And it's not like I normally wear a lot of makeup. Usually the only time I wear a ton of it is when I'm having a day when I know I look like crap.

I watch as the guys head back to start getting ready. Before Jasper gets up he hands me a box.

As I look down at the box that he handed me, my jaw drops. It's a one terabyte external drive. I only mentioned I wanted to get one, he didn't need to get one for me. I glance back toward the back, gaping before looking back at the box. Shaking my head, I put the box down next to my computer and finish getting ready.

I'm packing up my makeup when Lucius slides in next to me, putting his arm around me to pull me into his side. I glance up at him, his ice blue eyes bright as he holds me to him.

"What a pair of lovesick puppies," Nicholai teases, as he passes us. "I can't wait for the honeymoon phase to be over."

I look at Nicholai, smiling. "Maybe you just need to get a woman, rather than the jail-bait you hook up with." It's well known that Nic usually hooks up with younger girls who I'd consider barely legal.

"Ouch, Toni, you sure know where to hit a guy," Nic returns, holding his hands to his heart as if I've wounded him.

I laugh. "Aww, Nic can't take ribbing from a woman?" Lucius's chest rumbles as he chuckles quietly. I just hope that if I cross a line with teasing that someone tells me, rather than getting pissed off with me.

Nicholai laughs. "You'll definitely fit in with us, Toni."

Chapter Nineteen
TONI

After the show, when we're all back on the bus, I enjoy sitting and hanging out with the guys. Once I've finished doing some of my work, I relax with a beer and chat with them. What surprises me is that Lucius stays up with us, probably because he wants to stay awake until I'm ready to head to bed, or maybe he just wants to enjoy some time with the guys.

"Nicholai, what's one of the pranks you pulled that backfired?" I ask, knowing they love to play pranks. I was thankful I had yet to be pranked. I know my time will come; a right of passage into their fold when they decide I'm truly one of them.

"Chris and I had put hair remover in Luc and Al's body wash, only to have them swap the bottles with ours. We ended up losing chunks of our body hair."

I laugh. "I guess that served you right."

Chris replies, "Oh, yeah. We stopped with the pranks like that. We thought about putting hair dye in your shampoo and conditioner but figured Luc would kill us if we did."

"You got that right," Luc replies.

I'm starting to get tired and figure it is time to head to bed. Leaning into Luc I whisper, "I'm ready to go to bed."

He growls quietly into my ear, "Thank fuck! Let's go!"

"Well, I'm off to bed. Have a good night, guys," I say, as I make my way to the bedroom with Luc following me.

I know both of us are tired, so I strip down, climb into bed next to Luc, and cuddle into him, lulled to sleep by the beat of his heart beneath my ear.

Light is streaming in when I hear a chuckle that stirs me awake. Somehow during the night I've rolled to my back, away from Luc while he slept on his stomach. Pulling my right arm away to rub the sleep from my eyes, I find that I can't. I go to move my left arm and find it hard to move. As I blink the sleep away I glance down.

"What the fuck," I mutter. Hearing snickering, I glance up to see both Chris and Nic grinning and hear the click of the camera Chris is holding. "What the fuck," I yell this time. The sheets are tangled around me and my upper body is bared, Luc's back is exposed and one of his legs freed from the sheet.

My right arm is tied to the headboard while my left arm is tied to Luc's left arm. I keep trying to pull on my left arm only to feel the material starting to dig into my wrist. I can't help but panic as a memory hits me.

I was only eleven or so and had just been placed with my fifth foster family within the last year. They had wanted a boy, but instead got me, not hiding their disappointment over me being a girl. I was stuck being treated like a slave to the family, beaten when they thought I'd done something wrong. I tried to be a good girl, but tonight I was getting in trouble for something I didn't do. My foster brother lied, saying I broke the vase that he smashed on purpose.

I found myself being tied to the bed with coarse rope that was sure to chafe my delicate skin. He liked when I was left with marks. Danny, their son, was sitting on me in order to hold me down while my foster father was tying me to the bed face down. I could barely breathe under his weight.

Once my arms and legs were tied to the bedposts, Danny got off me and yanked my pants down. I screamed, telling them to stop. They both laughed maniacally. I can hear the rustling as Mr. Maxwell pulls his belt from his pants.

I scream at the first strike against my bare skin, the leather of the belt abrading my flesh. The burning pain is all I feel with hit after hit. I can't help but try to squirm as tears fall, wanting to get out, but the rope is tightening around my skin, making my hands and feet tingle as numbness sets in.

I'm crying so hard I can't hear what they are saying. I want to retreat into myself, find a safe place away from the horror I have to endure. Wishing I had a family who treated me better, wishing I'd never been born. It's not the first time they've beaten me, and I know it won't be the last. Both father and son are enjoying the pain being inflicted upon me.

"Stop struggling, Toni," Chris hisses,

pulling me from my past. "The prank is more for Luc than you. He'll get you loose as soon as he wakes."

I watch helplessly as they back out of the bedroom, snickering. I try to calm myself down, but it's no use, I can't help but panic. Nic and Chris are just trying to prank us, not hurt me. But my panic isn't letting me see clearly. I need to get loose.

Shouldering Luc, I say through clenched teeth, "Wake up Lucius. Those fuckers are gonna get a beat down!" I'm trying to fight back the anxiety that being tied up gives me, but every moment that I'm immobile brings me closer to losing it.

Luc groans, "Go back to sleep, baby."

"Luc, we're tied to the bed. They have a picture of me half naked!" I practically scream at him.

He turns his head to me. "Say what?"

I go to pull on my left arm to show him, but due to the angles our arms are in I can't pull much. "Luc, Nic and Chris tied us to the bed. My left arm is tied to yours and my right is tied to the bed."

Trying to push himself up I notice when he realizes he's tied too. "Those fuckers."

I watch as he keeps pulling on his right arm. It's tied to the bed frame below the mattress. It's not long before I hear material rip, telling me his arm is free. It takes him a few moments to figure out how to maneuver so that he can free his other arm without hurting me.

As he moves carefully to not hurt either of us, I watch as he brings our wrists up. It's then that I realize it's a pair of my underwear that was used to tie us together. With his free hand, he makes quick work of getting our arms untied.

With my left arm free, I try to move up the bed to make it easier for Luc to loosen my right arm. Once free, I watch as he throws on a pair of boxers before storming out the door. I pull on a pair of shorts and a tank top as I follow suit. I'm so angry I want to cry, but I want to make them pay first.

"Where's the camera?" Luc bellows, as I make my way down the hallway between the bunks.

Coming up behind him, I can see both Chris and Nic smirking while Nic replies, "It's been put away for safekeeping."

My body is quaking in anger, of feeling not only violated by what the pair of them did, but also from what happened to me in my past. My blood boils and I want to hit someone or something. I feel embarrassed that they saw me panicking; I don't want them to know the broken me. I hate that after all these years the abuse I was subjected to still affects me the way that it does.

I push past Luc and slap both Nic and Chris. "Where the fuck is the camera? No one is gonna see that picture!"

"Fine, it's in my bunk," Chris says, pouting like a child.

Luc goes to the bunk and pulls out the phone, scrolling through to delete the picture.

"You ever do that again I'll chop off your nuts and mount them to the side of the bus," I threaten, as I glare at both of them. I really want to hit them again.

They both chuckle before Luc decks them both, effectively shutting them up.

"I ever catch you with a picture of Toni in any state of undress, I'll let her do it," Luc hisses before storming off back to the bedroom.

"We're sorry, Toni," Nic says contritely.

"You crossed the line with that prank. And using my underwear? Fuck, Luc just ruined a pair. What were you thinking?"

"We thought it would be funny," Chris replies.

I hold up my arm to show them the welt growing on my wrist. "You think this is funny? Luc has one too."

"You wouldn't have the welts if you didn't struggle so much," replies Nic.

"You fucking tied me up!" I holler, as I smack him again.

Jasper comes from the bunks rubbing his eyes in a pair of tight white boxers. "What's with all the yelling?"

"Ask these two knuckleheads," I reply, as I push past him to head to the bedroom to try and cool off. I don't even care that I shoved him out of my way.

As I close the door softly behind me, I watch as Luc plays with his phone. I sit next to him, leaning my head on his shoulder. "I can't believe they did that."

"It's not that bad of a pic," he says, as he shows me.

"Oh my God, I hope they didn't post that."

"You look good tied up, we should try it sometime," he replies with a smirk.

I giggle. "Luc, there is no way I'm letting you tie me up after that. Even if they didn't do that, it's something I'd never be able to handle."

Pulling me so that I'm straddling him, he kisses my lips before slowly kissing his way to my neck. Between kisses he says, "But what if it's something I want to try? Having you at my mercy to pleasure."

"You don't need me tied for that. All you have to do is touch me and I'm at your mercy," I moan.

My anger dissolves into desire. This is how much this man affects me. How he can transform my emotions in an instant.

Chapter Twenty

TONI

ONE NIGHT AFTER A SHOW I FIND MYSELF restless. Luc is fast asleep next to me, but sleep evades me. It's only been a few days that I've been on tour with the guys, and I feel comfortable around them. I quickly slip from the bed, pulling on a pair of sweatpants and a hoodie.

I make my way toward the kitchen, figuring that maybe I can get some work done. The guys are all in bed, so I quietly turn on my notebook, the screen providing just enough light for me to type by, compared to using my tablet. To make sure I don't wake anyone, I grab my headphones and move with my notebook over to the loveseat, hoping it's far enough from where the guys are sleeping.

I turn on some music to listen to as I work

and begin sorting through the pictures I took today, smirking at a few of the candid shots I got. A lot of them are of the guys joking around backstage, while others are of them deep in thought while waiting for the opener to finish so they can take the stage. I know these are one's that they won't want shared with the general public, so I post them on their personal pages for their friends and family to see.

I start editing the rest of the pictures to clean them up before posting them to the group and individual pages. I have fun captioning them as I post and hope they don't get mad at me for what I'm writing.

I nearly jump when I find Jas taking a seat next to me. When we've worked together we usually sat side by side. I'm more comfortable around him than I was before, but I still feel awkward around him on occasion when I'm feeling vulnerable.

"Hey," I say quietly, pulling off my headphones.

"Can't sleep?" he asks.

I shake my head as I answer, "No. I don't know why either. Just feeling restless."

"Comes with the territory when you're stuck on the bus and not used to it."

"It's not that. I think it mostly has to do with how I grew up. For years I survived on only a little bit of sleep."

"Why would you have to survive on a little bit of sleep?"

I'm not sure if I want to tell Jasper about my past, especially with the fact that we have a shared history that he may not even remember. But if I want him to open up to me about his past, then maybe I need to open up to him about mine.

With a sigh, I answer. "From the age of ten, I was in foster care. For years, I bounced from home to home, and let's just say I hated it. It wasn't until I was with my last foster family, when I started high school, did I get a family that actually cared about me. They even adopted me. But I went through a lot of abusive situations with most of the families I was placed with. Because I never knew when something would happen, I would stay awake as long as I could."

"Why were you in foster care?"

"I was taken away from my mom. She was deemed unfit to care for me."

"That sucks," he says.

"Yeah, my life did for a while. But there's something I've been wanting to ask you for a while now but haven't had the privacy to be able to."

His expression changes, as if he's wondering what I want to ask him about with no one else around. "What?"

Swallowing in order to give me an extra moment, I then push on. "Um. I don't know how to say or ask this."

"Just say it."

"Do you remember going to a party in the spring the year before Luc noticed me at the bar?"

He chuckles. "Springtime back then was a time I usually found myself drinking a fair amount, so hitting parties was a normal thing. I don't remember a whole lot. Why do you ask?"

Blushing, I say, "I met you at a party that spring. You weren't with the guys. I only went because Keri dragged me out for my seventeenth birthday."

"I wish I could tell you I remembered meeting you."

"So, you don't remember that we..." I pause, knowing I'm blushing even more. "That we slept together?"

"We what?" he asks, confused.

"Keri's goal was to get me drunk for my birthday and to pop my cherry. What she didn't know was that I had already had sex. Anyway, we were a few of the youngest people at the party, and she succeeded in getting me drunk. I didn't know anyone there except for Keri, and she kept taking off to try to find a guy for me. I saw you sitting by yourself drinking and ended up hanging out with you. We talked a little, and because Keri had been pressuring me to pick someone to sleep with, I asked you. We were both drunk, but you agreed. We locked ourselves in the bathroom and you fucked me."

"Fuck, Toni, I don't remember that. I'm sorry, that should never have happened. Being drunk is no excuse for letting that happen."

"I don't want to make this awkward for us. But I wasn't sure if you remembered or not. Even Keri doesn't know that I slept with you, and I haven't told Luc either. I don't want something that happened before I was interested in him to come between anyone. I had hoped that maybe you just didn't recognize me when I saw you almost a year later and then now."

"Shit, Toni. I really don't remember. Springtime was rough for me back then. I'd be drunk for days. Fuck, this makes me sound like an asshole."

"You're not an asshole, Jasper. I'm the one who came on to you. And you deserve to know that we have some history. I just hope you don't think I'm some slut who sleeps around."

He smirks. "Toni, I can't picture you being the type to sleep around. To me it sounds like what happened between us was out of character for both of us."

I grin. "It definitely was. I drank enough to let my inhibitions go that night. I just hope you don't mind me bringing it up."

"I'm glad you told me. You're stuck with us for a month, and the last thing we want is for you to be uncomfortable with any of us. It's something that happened in the past and we can leave it there."

Wow, this went better than I expected. Here I thought it would be awkward. It might be, but if he can look past it, then so can I. "I just don't know if I should tell Luc about it or not. I don't want to make it weird between the two of you."

"If you tell him, I can always talk to him afterward to smooth things out. I'm sure he'll understand that it's in the past. Don't get me wrong, Toni, you're an attractive woman, but I'm not interested in you that way."

I grin. "The feeling is mutual, Jas. I like you as a friend now that I've gotten to know you a little better than I did before."

He chuckles. "Good, then we won't let it affect us."

I feel better having talked to Jas. And I'm glad we can move forward as friends, rather than let what happened between us get in the way of things. He's definitely going to be a catch for someone someday. I just hope when I confess to Luc, he won't feel threatened by my past with Jas.

Our conversation switches over to what I was doing when he came out to join me before we both finally head to our respective beds.

When I crawl back into bed with Luc, I drift off to sleep easily, a weight having been lifted.

Chapter Twenty-One
TONI

EVERY NIGHT AFTER A SHOW, I SPEND TIME posting pictures on the social media sites, with Jasper's help captioning them. Our night talking about the secret I'm hiding from Luc is something we've put behind us; my honesty with Jas opening a doorway to our friendship. There are nights when I slip from bed with Luc just to spend time with Jasper because I can't sleep and he's usually awake.

We sit and talk quietly while we work. He opens up to me about a lot of things, most of which he wants me to keep private. I learn that his dad walked out on them when he and Jade were ten, and their mom was rarely around because she was working so much in order to provide for them. When he became old enough, he and his sister both got jobs that worked around their school hours.

He got a job at a music store and was able to spend a lot of time playing instruments. He could play almost everything. But out of the members of the band, he was better at drums, though he did like to play guitar. When I think about it, Jasper would have made an awesome front man. He's gorgeous, and I know enough fans drool over him. Not that Nic doesn't have his fair share of fans.

"Jas, can I ask you something personal?" I ask shyly.

"Maybe," he replies.

"How come you never mention girlfriends? I'm sure you've had some."

"Not since high school. When Isabelle died before we graduated, I was left devastated. If it weren't for the guys, I'm not sure where I'd be right now. They saved me from going down a darker path than what I was already following."

"Who's Isabelle?"

"She was my high school sweetheart. We met our first year of high school. She was one of the most popular girls in school. The moment I saw her, I wanted her. She had golden blonde hair that she always wore up because she played sports. But it was her gray eyes that drew me in. When she was in a good mood they reminded me of an overcast sky, but in a bad mood they were like a thunderstorm cloud. I could stare into her eyes all day. Within months she was my girlfriend. She was my first for a lot of things."

"Like?"

"She was the first girl I kissed. The first girl I had sex with. The first and only girl I loved."

"What happened to her?"

"At first, she got sick. She just thought it was a cold that was hanging around. I finally managed to convince her to go see the doctor. She had a chest infection, which then turned into pneumonia. She was so weak from her body trying to fight the infection, along with the medication she was on. Then she was hit with sepsis from a cut that got infected. Her body couldn't fight both the pneumonia and the sepsis, and eventually it just stopped fighting."

"I'm so sorry, Jas," I say, as tears slip down my face. My chest tightens at the thought of how heartbroken he must have been. Realization hits me of why he didn't remember me from that first night we met at the party. He was drinking away his pain.

"For months I watched her get sicker and sicker. And there wasn't a damn thing I could do to help her. I missed her so much that I tried to join her. It was then that the guys really banded around me and helped pull me through the dark days I had. Between them and a friend I met on a suicide survivor chat site, Cami, they made me see I had more to live for. I got the tattoo on my shoulder for Isabelle, as a way to remind myself of her and what I've been through."

"You never talk about friends."

"As you notice, Toni, I usually keep to myself. But Cami kept prying, asking me to open up to her. After a while, she told me she couldn't keep our friendship going if I didn't give her something. So, I started opening up to her more. Sure, she knew about Isabelle and what I went through, but I never gave her anything else."

"So, Cami is making you open up to her?"

"Yeah. A year after we signed with the label I told her who I was, but I made her guess a little first. From then on, I've begged her to meet me, but she's refused. She gets panic attacks at the thought of it. She's been through a rough life."

"And I bet you've helped her as much as she's allowed."

"I have. I keep offering more, but she refuses. While she was in college, I'd replace her phone and computer with a new one before the beginning of the year. She graduated two years ago and she's refused to let me keep replacing her phone, but I still pay the phone bill."

"So, you've never met her?"

"Nope. But I want to. She's one of my best friends, outside of the guys. When something amazing happens, she's the first one I want to tell."

"Aww, Jas. Maybe one day she'll come around and you can finally meet her. I'm sorry about what happened to Isabelle."

"I hope one day Cami does come around. "

I wrap my arm around Jas in an awkward hug, given the position we are sitting in. He wraps his arm around me, returning the hug.

"You'll find someone one day, Jas, I just can't tell you exactly when. Maybe it's Cami, maybe not. But whoever she is, she'll have me to deal with if she hurts you. I may be with Luc, but it doesn't mean I don't love you and the rest of the guys. You're all like family to me. Luc changed me from being the shy loner and made me take a chance on opening myself up. Him making me open up has allowed me to be closer to my adoptive family, something they're very thankful for."

"You're like a sister to me too, Toni. And you're a lot less annoying than Jade," he replies with a chuckle.

"Well, I'll take that as a compliment," I say with a laugh.

Chapter Twenty-Two
LUCIUS

I SIT IN THE CHAIR AT THE DESK, WEARING MY headphones, which are connected to my practice amp. With my electric blue Superstrat guitar across my lap, I'm working on trying to perfect the solo for a song we want on our next album, but I just can't seem to find the right notes. I've been stuck with finding the right balance to it for weeks. Toni's asleep in bed; we had an eventful day yesterday, having to move hotels. I wanted her to get some rest, knowing that later we'll be going out. Today we're free to do what we want, I want to take her out to see the city. I just want to have time to act like a regular couple, carefree and enjoying the moment.

Glancing toward the bed, I can't help the grin that spreads across my face. Her hair in disarray from both sleep and sex. She looks content, peaceful even, with both her hands resting under her cheek. The sheets tangled around her body, hiding the curves I've come to love. I want more days like this with her. Knowing we have roughly two weeks left together makes me feel unsettled; I don't want her to leave. I know my heart belongs to her, like an invisible string is tied from mine to hers. I don't want to lose her. I'd do damn near anything to make her happy.

I set my guitar on it's stand and turn off my amp while pulling off my headphones. Standing, I stretch before walking toward the bed. I lay down facing her and watch her sleep. A smile tugs at her lips as she releases a soft sigh. It's almost as if she senses I'm near.

As I watch her, I'm tempted to wake her. I don't, though. I love being able to watch her sleep, especially when she's in a deep sleep and oblivious to the world around her. I can tell when she's dreaming, both good and bad.

Today is going to be an interesting day. Hopefully I can pull it off without a hitch. Toni doesn't know it, but I started planning today's agenda as soon as I knew we'd have some free time for ourselves. I made sure the guys knew today is to be a day where I get to spend some much needed alone time with my woman. I've shelled out a small fortune for what I have planned, but it'll be worth it in the end.

I smirk when Toni groans, trying to wedge her head between the pillows. The drapes in our hotel room don't do much to hide the brightness of the sun outside. I'm always awake before she is. Having started the habit of staying up late at night, she prefers to sleep in. Some days I let her sleep in peace by going to the front of the bus, and others, I stay in bed, waiting for her to wake. Our rare stays in hotels, I tend to try to let her sleep. Other times I wake her because I don't want to wait. I've had to learn to be creative when waking her, as her grumpiness is not something I like to see.

Toni lifts her head from between the pillows, then looks at me before groaning and dropping her head back where it was. I unsuccessfully try to suppress a chuckle, earning a glare from her. As grumpy as she may look, she's still cute.

"Don't you have something better to do than watch me sleep?" Her voice is raspy from sleep.

"It's one of my favorite pastimes." My smirk earns me a scowl. Little does she know that I spend moments in the morning while she sleeps watching her. Every morning, I begrudgingly leave her, knowing she needs her sleep after her late nights with Jas. But there are rare times, like today, I don't have to leave her.

"Ugh, why do you have to be such a morning person? You'd think that you'd be a night owl like the rest of us."

I chuckle. It's not that I'm a morning person, the fact that I'm asleep before the others is why I'm up earlier. Nic, on occasion, is awake around the same time as me or earlier, he's always been one who doesn't sleep much.

I brush stray strands of hair from her face. "I'm going to order us breakfast. Why don't you take a shower so we can start getting ready, I have a fun day planned for us."

"You mean we're not spending the day with everyone else?" she asks, sounding hopeful, her eyes glittering.

"No, just the two of us today."

Her excited smile is bright, transforming her

face from sleepy to radiant. It's a smile I want to see on her daily. Pushing the covers from her body, she climbs from the bed, heading to the bathroom. I watch the sway of her hips, totally ogling her ass as she walks. I adjust my cock in my boxers before getting up to call room service.

When Toni emerges from the bathroom with a towel around her body, I've already pulled on a pair of jeans and am in the process of pulling on a t-shirt. I can tell she's excited by the smile she wears and the bounce in her step.

While she's getting dressed, room service arrives. We eat quietly. I'm nervous about what she will think about what I've planned. We've never really talked about what types of things she likes to do for dates. But I don't want to do typical things. I want her to experience things that she'll always remember.

When we're through eating, we finish getting ready to leave. I've already given our car service the itinerary for today so everything we do will be a surprise. I don't want Toni to know anything we're doing until we get there.

The car drives us to the airport that houses the helicopter tour I've booked. Toni's eyes widen as we arrive.

"Where are we going?" she asks.

"Wait and see." Taking her hand, I lead her toward the building so we can check in. I pay the extra fees, and all the while Toni is grinning.

We sit in the uncomfortable plastic chairs in the waiting room. Toni leans against me and checks her phone. She reads an email from her boss regarding her last update yielding some good information and saying that he looks forward to the next update.

Pulling away, she turns to me. "I'm supposed to be working, and here I am, slacking off by spending a day with you doing something fun."

I caress her cheek, and she closes her eyes as she leans into my touch. "Babe, you're allowed to have fun. You're not expected to work every day, yet you do. You deserve a day to relax and have a good time."

I watch as she takes a deep breath, pausing before exhaling. I wish I knew what was going on in her mind. I know she will feel like she doesn't deserve to be spoiled like I'm planning to do today. But will she regret everything I've done for her to make today special?

Opening her eyes, she smiles at me. "You're right. I've barely taken time to relax and enjoy myself. If it's not digging for the article, it's helping Jasper with social media. I deserve to have some time not working."

Sliding my hand behind her neck, I pull her to me, kissing her. I keep it brief, knowing she hates being caught in public. Her freak out in Toronto when we were photographed backstage was the first indication. She's tried to put distance between us when we've been in the public eye, something I don't let her get away with.

Our names are called. Taking her hand, we walk toward the woman who leads us outside where the helicopter waits. We're introduced to our pilot who is also the tour guide. We're helped into our harnesses once seated and then handed headsets.

Toni is excited, glancing all around, eyes wide as we begin flying through the sky. I barely register what the pilot says, my focus on Toni and the sights before us.

The twenty-five minute tour is over before I realize it. When we disembark the helicopter

Toni launches herself at me. "Oh my God, that was amazing!"

We head back to the car. Our next stop is the Statue of Liberty and a tour of Ellis Island. It's something that any tourists should do when in the city, and today is no exception. Wearing a ball cap and shades, I hope not to be recognized. I just want to enjoy today with my girl.

"You said that we're making a day of it. What else do you have planned?"

"You have to wait to find out." I smirk, knowing that she's not going to be happy being surprised as much as she will be today. But I'm taking pleasure in knowing that she's enjoying what I have planned.

When we get to the park where we're to meet up with the tour guide, Toni pulls on my hand. Her voice is panicked as she asks, "What happens if you're recognized?"

I pull her close and whisper, "You don't think I wouldn't have planned to make sure we had security with us? They're here in plain clothes."

"When did you start planning this, and how did you hide it from me?"

"As soon as I knew what days we had free I started to plan it. I made sure to book everything when you were busy or asleep. I wanted it to be a complete surprise for you. I told the guys that I wanted to spend a whole day with you alone, since we don't get much time to ourselves."

"I can't believe you planned all this just so we can get time to ourselves!" She curls into my side, allowing me to wrap my arms around her shoulders.

By the time we make it back to the hotel we're exhausted. I'm shocked that we managed to make it the whole day without me being recognized, but we did. Toni let me take some selfies of us to post, so her family can see, but mostly for the memories.

With how much fun we had, I'm more than convinced that Toni is definitely the one for me, that we're tied to one another. I know it'll take a hell of a lot to break the strings that hold us together.

Each surprise I revealed today, I know Toni

was happy and excited about. I just hope she knows that she's worth spoiling; that she'll take the chance to go all in. I know she's not used to being spoiled much, but I will do anything to make her happy, even if it means having to leave the band. Part of me is hoping she'll stay on and take over most of our social media for us.

Toni groans the moment she kicks her feet free from her shoes. We did a fair amount of walking downtown. It was nice to just enjoy ourselves, to pretend like we were vacationers. Several times Toni surprised me in uncharacteristic displays of affection, usually when we did something fun. Window shopping wasn't at the top of my list, but Toni enjoyed it. My bank account, not so much. At a jewelry store, I bought a necklace I'd seen Toni admiring before balking at the price. It was white gold with interconnecting hearts on a thin chain.

Taking her hand, I lead her to the bed. Sitting down, I have her settle between my legs. "Close your eyes," I order. When she complies, I remove the necklace from my pocket and put it on her, kissing her bare neck when done. "Open them," I whisper in her ear.

Her hand flies up to the necklace, her eyes widening before standing to look in the mirror. While she does, I pull off my boots, knowing she needs to process the gift.

"Luc," she calls softly. Lifting my gaze to her I can see the anguish in her eyes. "It's too much."

Standing, I walk toward her. Tilting her head to look at me, I tell her, "It's a gift. Get used to it, baby. I like being able to spoil you. You deserve it."

"But it cost..."

"I don't care about price tags, Toni. I saw how much you liked it when you were looking at it." I don't care that I've cut her off, she needs to know that she's worth everything. Leaning down, I kiss her again, effectively quieting her.

A knock on our door pulls us apart. I begrudgingly leave her to answer. Al stands on the other side holding a bag out for me. I'd sent him on an errand for me when an idea struck me. "Thanks," I say before closing the door.

Grinning, I turn back to Toni who's admiring her necklace in the mirror again.

Slipping my hand into the bag, I pull out the tissue wrapped item. Pulling the paper from it, I smile when I see it. He had to go to SoHo just to find someone who could make it. It's distressed guitar strings entwined together, small beads holding together the twisted pieces. It's made into a heart-shaped bracelet. I hope she loves the twisted heartstrings.

Walking to her, I take her hand and slip the bracelet on her wrist. Her eyes shoot from the bracelet to mine and back. Lifting her arm, she admires the bracelet. Smiling, she throws herself at me. "It's so beautiful and thoughtful!"

"I hoped you'd like it. When I figured out you liked hearts I wanted to surprise you with this, a way for you to always keep me close. They're strings from one of my guitars."

The way she beams at me let's me know I made the right choice with this gift. I'll have to remember that it's the thoughtful ones she likes better. I thought about getting her one of those charm bracelets, but I doubt we'd be able to find charms that represent places we see.

"I love the bracelet," she says, pulling me from my thoughts. Leaning up on the tips of her toes, she kisses me. I deepen the kiss, lifting her

from her feet and wrapping her legs around my
waist.

Chapter Twenty-Three

TONI

MY MONTH WITH THE GUYS FLIES BY QUICKLY. It was more than I could have hoped for. I've spent a lot of time helping Jasper with their social media accounts. And the venue pictures I take bring a rush of people to their fan pages, with new members joining after every show to tag themselves at the events. My bosses are ecstatic with how much information I have gathered for the article. The guys were able to hook me up with talking to their families online to get information as well--some embarrassing stories from their youth along with childhood photographs.

Mrs. Black has demanded I come down for dinner one weekend when I get back so she can meet the new woman in her son's life. She's been curious about me, since it's been everywhere that Lucius and I are together. Apparently, Alucard has raved about how well Luc and I get along and how happy he is.

Nikki has been stirring the pot online every chance she gets. There are a few fans who are raising a stink about our relationship, and my own inbox has been blowing up with nasty messages. But I don't care; it's a price I have to pay to be with him. My association with him has brought me into notoriety, being that I stole the heart of a man whom so many others wanted.

We're in Florida by the time my month is up, and thankfully, on my last day we don't have to travel anywhere. They don't have to be back on the road until the following morning after my flight leaves. Lucius and I ditch everyone to spend some time alone together. He takes me to one of the beaches, where we go for a walk along the surf. The trunks he has on only enhance his body, especially with the way they hang off his hips. I feel self-conscious in the skimpy bikini we picked up for me; it's revealing more of my body than I want to. When his hungry eyes take me in, I've never felt more beautiful, desired even.

We don't talk much as he holds my hand while we walk. I know his thoughts are similar to mine, neither of us wanting me to leave. But I have to get back to work. Jasper and I had talked one night when I couldn't sleep about me staying on and handling their social media like I have been. It's something I have enjoyed and will miss doing. He knows I plan to try to keep helping with it while I'm home. The least I can do is answer some of the fan questions.

We make our way back to where we left our stuff on the beach and decide to lay on the sand. I lay on my stomach with my feet in the air, staring at Lucius. I can never get enough of looking at him. He lays on his side with his fingers running lightly up and down my back, sending shivers across my body.

"Have you thought about taking Jasper up on the offer to keep working for us?" he asks finally.

"I have, but if I do, I need to tie up some loose ends at home before I can think about committing to it," I reply. "But I need to think about it some more. I don't want to make the decision to do it because I don't want to leave you or because I'm lonely without you. And I don't want the guys mad that I'm hanging around all the time."

"They won't be mad. They'll probably miss you as much as I will. They've had fun with you hanging around. They think of you as one of us."

"Won't you be sick of me being around you all the time?" I ask. Even after this month of being together, I still can't help but feel insecure about our relationship. I know I love him, but I haven't told him how I felt and he hasn't said anything either.

"I could never be sick of you. When we get to Vegas we could always get married." His grin is teasing, contradicting his serious tone.

I blush furiously, shocked that he would even suggest marriage when he hasn't said the words that I've wanted to hear from him more than anything.

"If I were to get married, I'd want my family to be there for it." The email I sent them when Luc and I got together brought us closer. I talk to them almost daily whether it's a phone call, text, or email. They're happy to see me being happy.

"We could fly them in for it. We have a couple of shows and then a few days off in Vegas."

"You're serious?" I ask, shock evident in my voice and on my face as I look at him.

"Yes, I told you before I knew where I wanted this to go."

His eyes are intense and serious as I look into them, mesmerized. I swallow. He wants to marry me, like really marry me. "Lucius, I don't know what to say."

"Say that you'll at least think about it. We have a few weeks before we get to Vegas, but we can pull it off. Once the tour is done, we can take off someplace for our honeymoon or plan to do a wedding our families are involved with."

"I promise I'll think about it," I reply. My head is spinning. He still hasn't said the words, but what he's proposing must mean it's how he feels about me.

Smiling, he leans toward me and kisses me. Even though it's not deep or intense, I can still feel the stirrings of desire. I sigh into his mouth, knowing that he will always have this effect on me.

"So, how are you going to fill your time once I leave?" I ask, hoping to lighten the mood.

His eyes darken. "If it's not too late after the shows, I hope to spend the time talking to you. I know I won't be able to talk to you throughout the day if you're working."

"Yeah, my boss would probably get pissed if I spent all my time talking to you rather than focusing on doing my job. I know they're happy with what I've managed to gather for them for the article, though."

A ringing sound cuts through the air and Lucius groans as he fishes his phone from the pocket of his board shorts. Looking at it, he curses and types back.

"What's wrong?" I ask.

"Jasper just texted that some fans have recognized me here and have posted pictures of us, giving away our location"

"Shit, we should get out of here before we get mobbed," I say. Getting time alone has been difficult for us; we're always spotted, no matter how low profile we try to be.

"Yeah, it won't be long before that happens."

As he stands, he reaches down for my hand to help me up. Gathering the towels that we brought from the hotel, we head back to the car we rented.

I know Lucius doesn't mind taking time for fans, but I also know he doesn't want to have to share what is our last day together. I know I don't want to have to share him either; it's why I was glad he suggested we take off by ourselves. We've only had short stints of time alone in the past month, usually when we get to a city early enough that we have time to go do something before the show. Of the cities we've been to, New York was my favourite by far. We were able to be tourists and go see a few of the sights that I'd heard about but never got to see the last time I had been there.

At the car, I pull on the summer dress I bought to wear with the bathing suit while he pulls on his t-shirt. It's a shame that he's covering his sculpted body. I know firsthand the hardness of his chest and every contour of his delicious frame. I've learned every spot to lick, kiss, touch, and nibble that turns him on and makes him lose control. And just as I make him lose control, he does the same to me, mastering my body with a single look or touch.

I don't share with anyone the insecurities I have about leaving, and I hope it doesn't show on my face when they hit me. I fear that while on tour, when I'm not with them, that Lucius will meet another woman who will turn his head. One who would take him from me. Though I know he's loyal, I can't help but wonder if he would leave me for another woman. He's never shown other women any attention, other than signing autographs and posing for pictures--even posing he will look at me and smile for me. He's never given any reason for me to be insecure, but I just can't stop it from happening.

The GPS in the rental gives us directions back to the hotel. Lucius and I both grow quiet, lost in our own thoughts. I know tonight he wants to take me out for dinner on a rare date, with real food. Most of our meals have been fast food. The guys find time to work out to keep in shape, and I've even joined in with trying to keep the weight off from the unhealthy eating lifestyle we've grown accustomed to.

We leave the car with the parking attendant

at the hotel and make our way back to our room. It's still early, considering we've only managed to get to spend a few short hours at the beach. There isn't much we can do without attracting attention, so I was kind of shocked we managed to get as much time in at the beach as we did.

Once the door to our room closes, I'm pressed against the wall with Lucius kissing me hungrily. His tongue runs my lower lip, seeking entrance. I sigh, letting him in to deepen the kiss. I can feel the hem of my dress being lifted and his fingers pulling on the ties of the bikini bottoms. Before I even realize it, he has his shorts shoved down low enough to release his hard member and I'm being lifted and impaled on him.

Gasping, I realize that we're skin to skin. We've been careful, even with me on birth control, to always use condoms when we make love. This will be the first time he hasn't bothered with one.

"Fuck, baby, you feel so good," he moans against my lips.

With my legs wrapped around his waist, he drives into me with enough force that I can't control the sounds coming from my mouth. His pace is fast, as if he seeks a quick release. Slipping a hand from around his neck, I reach under my skirt to rub myself, trying to bring my release to push us both over the edge.

Most of the time when Lucius makes love to me I never know if it will be hard and fast or slow and tender. It's always a surprise, and more often than not we are left either wanting more of one another or completely sated, yet still wanting more.

As my release rocks my body, I bite into his neck to keep from screaming. He grunts as he empties his seed into me, gently rocking it out. Part of me fears getting pregnant, and a part of me hopes that I will. I fear I would never be able to be the parent a child deserves. But a small part of me wouldn't mind having a little reminder of Lucius if we were to ever to not be together.

Pulling away from the wall, Lucius carries me through the bedroom into the bathroom before setting me on the counter. He turns on the shower, stripping his clothes off before stripping me of mine. Leading me into the shower, he washes me gently from head to toe, licking and kissing me everywhere, including bringing me to another orgasm that makes me feel boneless. Not wanting to leave him hanging, I return the favour, knowing how much he loves having my mouth on him.

We spend the remainder of our afternoon lying in bed naked, talking, touching, and kissing. I almost want to call to cancel my flight so I can stay. But I know I need to get home and back to work. My boss is already hinting that I'll be going out on assignment the following week to meet with another band to do research on them; I was going to be delving into their childhood. Usually an assignment like that means I'll be gone for a while, and I wasn't sure where they're sending me because they haven't given me any details. I had hoped that I could at least take the weekend and go home to visit my family and live up to my promise to visit Mrs. Black.

"Let's order in," I suggest. I don't want to go out and chance getting recognized by the public. I want to be selfish and keep Lucius to myself, even if I feel bad that we're not spending any time with the guys before I leave.

He chuckles. "I want to take you out, baby. It's not like we've gotten to go out much while you've been with us. I want to at least take you on a date before you have to go."

I smile at his sweetness. "But I want to be selfish and keep you to myself. You know you'll get recognized anywhere we go."

"Up, and get ready," he says, lightly smacking my ass.

Pouting, I do as he says. I pull out a pair of black lace matching underwear and root through my bag for my little black dress. I pull out the only pair of heels that I brought, which haven't been worn until now. As I get dressed, I peek over and see him pulling on a pair of dark washed jeans and a tight-fitting t-shirt. I quickly pull my hair into a messy bun and apply some makeup.

I find myself smiling as we make our way down to the lobby. As much as I want to keep him to myself tonight, it is nice to be able to actually go on a date. I just hope we don't run into fans who will interrupt us too much. Thankfully, fans haven't figured out what hotel we're staying in like they did in New York. It was so bad there, we had to change hotels.

At the restaurant, Lucius takes my hand as we are led to our table. He reserved a table for us earlier, so we'd have one waiting for us. We're getting a few looks as we pass through the dining room. I know we make an odd couple, especially with me dressed up and him in jeans and a t-shirt. Or it could be our physical differences, his dark features to my light. Or they could have recognized who he is and wondered what he's doing with an average girl like me.

For the most part, we're left alone during our dinner. Our table is at the back, in a kind of secluded nook. The lights are dim and candles flicker on every table, giving the room a romantic atmosphere. Lucius has made me feel special with each of our rare dates; he puts effort into what he plans for us. A few of them have been private tours to various places he thought I might like. That alone would have made me fall in love with him; being compatible is just a bonus.

My thoughts drift to Keri; we've barely spoken while I've been gone. Not for lack of trying. It's just that usually one of us is busy when the other is free. And there was no way I was sacrificing time with Lucius to talk to Keri, especially when it was times we were alone, with him rocking my world. I can't wait to be able to talk to Keri and get her advice on what I should do. I'm torn between a job I love and hope to advance in, or a job that will allow me to spend time with the man I love but would never get me anywhere.

I wasn't even sure if I would be able to handle the lifestyle they lead being on the road, and the various parties or events they have to attend. It's been easy this past month because it's short term, but tours can last months on end. Then there is the time working on new material, recording, and of course making music videos, giving interviews, or last-minute changes to the agenda. We had to cut one of our dates short in Toronto so that he could go to a signing that had been planned at the last minute. I don't want to be the type of girlfriend who comes to resent what her man does for a living, knowing that he clearly loves it. Nor do I want a man to resent what I do for a living. It isn't fair to each other if that's the case.

After dinner, we make our way back to the hotel, and I can't help getting nervous. I want to tell him how I feel, to blurt out all my insecurities, but I don't want to ruin what will be our last night together for who knows how long.

Inside our room, he pulls me into his arms. "You're being awfully quiet tonight."

"Just thinking," I reply.

"About?"

Smiling at him, I say, "Us. What I want. What you say you want. What's the right thing to do? How can we make things work? Everything."

"Baby, I get that you can't make a decision yet. That you want some space to think about it. As much as I would love for you to stay and work for us, so that I can spend time with you, I know I can't force you to make a decision if you're not ready. Not like when I took matters into our hands to get you to come with us. This is something that you have to want, that will alter the course of our lives."

"Why do you have to be so patient?" I ask.

"I've waited six years for you, what's a little more time? Sure, I dated while I waited, I just didn't think I would ever run into you again."

"I wouldn't have been at the show if Keri didn't score the tickets. As much as I wanted to see the show, I just couldn't afford it when the tickets went on sale, and by the time I could afford them, they were sold out. So, we did luck out that Keri's friends couldn't go and sold her the tickets for cheap."

"You got the tickets for a reason. What's stopping you from staying? What can I help clear up?"

Taking a deep breath, I pull away slightly. "All you have said is that you want to marry me and that you would love for me to be able to stay. But you haven't said anything else."

"I do want to marry you. If you're waiting to hear me tell you that I love you, I was waiting until I knew you loved me before I told you that I did."

"You love me?"

"I didn't realize it when we were younger, but I do now. Having you settles me in a way no one has ever been able to. Holding you feels right."

"Lucius, I love you too." I begin to cry. He's

finally said the words I've been dying to hear, but he had to be prompted to say them rather than saying them because he wanted to.

"But?"

"I don't know how to be in a relationship. I don't know if I can handle your lifestyle." And I don't know if he'll still want me after he finds out about me and Jas.

"I think we've done fine with our relationship up to this point. As for our lifestyle, it's not as if we're like a lot of the other bands that get heavy into the drinking or drugs. Sure, we're on the road a lot, but that doesn't mean that it won't work."

"And what if you meet someone else?" I bite my lip, knowing I'm revealing my insecurity.

"There won't be anyone else, baby. You're it for me," he says, as he caresses my cheek, wiping the tears, before leaning down to kiss me.

His kiss is soft, and I want more. Pressing myself to him, I try to deepen the kiss. But he pulls away and I groan. I can't help the pout that appears. Smiling at me, he lifts me to him, and I wrap my legs around him. I don't care that my dress is riding up or that my shoes fall to the floor as he walks.

He arranges us so that he is sitting on the bed with his back against the headboard and me straddling him. "What else is bothering you?"

Dare I admit to him the secret I'm holding, or keep it to myself a little longer? What will he think when he finds out that I've been with one of his best friends? "I'm just being insecure, despite you not giving me any reason to be. I just can't help it. I don't feel like I'm good enough for you. You deserve someone who doesn't have the baggage I carry with me from my past. You should be with someone who wants to have a family with you, not someone who is terrified at the idea of having kids. You deserve someone who looks like a model, not someone who pretends to dress up nicely when they're more comfortable in a pair of sweats. Sure, I have to dress up to go to work, but that doesn't mean I have to like it."

"Of course I'd love to have kids someday, but if you don't, then that's fine with me, as long as I get you. Baggage is something everyone carries with them, just in different forms. I've come second to Alucard my whole life with being the baby of the family. You know he was born a whole three minutes before me? My own brother took pity on me as a child because I wasn't learning as fast as my twin. Do you know how hard it is to stand out as one of five kids? Just because I had loving parents doesn't mean that I don't have baggage from the family dynamics."

"I'm just scared that the lifestyle of you being on the road all the time will drive us apart."

"Baby, if you stay, you'd be with us every time we go. How else would you help Jasper with our social media? Sure, we'd have to give up the bedroom sometimes to the other guys, but they wouldn't care as long as we're happy."

"You make it sound so easy," I reply.

"It's as easy as we make it. Sure, we'll fight and want to have time away from one another, but what couple doesn't?"

"What about when you and the guys get sick of having me around all the time? I'm sure they'll eventually get tired of me constantly being on the road with you."

"They enjoy having you around. They like

that you can give as much as you take. It's nice having someone who actually fits in with us. It's easy for them to talk to you about anything, even though they try to keep the sex talk to a minimum. But they do that out of respect for you, not because they don't think you can hear it. They have respect for you because they know they can trust you with anything."

"It's not like they want to have their personal lives aired for the world to see. I know I don't want to share all of us with the world. Your on-stage persona of a badass is enough for me to share, I don't want to share the marshmallow inside."

"Did you just call me a marshmallow?" he asks, sounding amused.

"Yup, cuz you can be crusty on the outside as your badass rocker, and all gooey on the inside for me." I lean forward and kiss him as a way to distract him. I know no man wants to be called soft like a marshmallow.

"That is a comment we are not sharing with even the guys," he says with a growl and a chuckle.

"Wanna make a bet," I reply with a grin.

"They can rib you about it while I'm not here."

"Fuck me, they already rib me about not making you scream. I know I make you scream you just don't let them hear it."

"Did you not show them the bite marks I've left on you? That would be why I don't scream. If they really want me to scream, then I can try to not bite next time."

"Oh, they've seen the marks. They rib about that too."

"Aww, are you feeling like you're getting picked on?" I smirk, then pout at him.

"We pick on each other all the time, they're just enjoying watching a woman take me to my knees. Believe me, their time is coming, and when it does, payback is gonna be a bitch."

Changing the subject, I ask, "Do you think your family will like me?"

He chuckles before answering, "My mom already does. And if she does, then my dad will. My brothers may be a bit harder of a sell, but once they see how happy I am with you, they'll like you."

"My adopted mom is a little worried about me. She thinks I'm just a passing fancy for you.

Though she's happy with the fact that you've helped me connect with them."

"Parents just want what's best for their kids. Sometimes it takes them a bit to see that they're happy."

As we sit and talk, I can't help but wonder when we will be able to spend time together like this again, especially since knowing that after I get home I'll be sent out on assignment the following week. My boss likes to try to keep me busy and sometimes sends me on wild goose chases. There are a few of my research subjects for whom I had to travel to various different cities and towns for fact-finding missions.

The only sleep I manage to get during the night is a few quick cat naps. Lucius keeps waking me to make love. Thankfully, I'll be able to sleep on my flight from Tampa to Edmonton. I have to be at the airport at five a.m. for my eight a.m. flight. I'll have a quick layover in Minneapolis before connecting with my flight to Edmonton. My boss had been able to get me booked on United 5302, I just have to pick up my ticket at the airport.

At four o'clock, I drag myself out of bed

and have a quick shower. Thankfully, my stuff is already packed. I get dressed in a pair of form-fitting sweatpants and a t-shirt. When I fly, I want to be comfortable, especially since my trip home will be almost nine hours. It'll be almost three in the afternoon when I arrive in Edmonton. Keri is getting off early to come pick me up from the airport. I'm looking forward to getting to talk to her about everything that has happened this past month.

Lucius gets up with me and pulls on his typical dark jeans and a t-shirt. He's taking me to the airport to see me off. Helping me with my bags, we leave our room. I'm shocked to see all of the guys waiting outside our room.

"We wanted to see you off, but we won't all fit in the car so thought we'd say goodbye here," says Jasper, sounding sorrowful.

They each hug me in turn and tell me to have a good flight. I almost tear up at their thoughtfulness of wanting to see me off. I already know it will be hard leaving Lucius but saying goodbye to them is like saying goodbye to brothers I never had. They treat me as one of them, despite being a girl and dating one of them. I'm going to miss them, especially Jasper, as I've actually become closer to him than the rest, with all of the time we spent together working their social media. I would usually get up after Lucius fell asleep, and we'd sit at the table working and talking. I know Lucius isn't jealous of our bond; I've given no indication that we're anything more than friends, even if we have history he still doesn't know about. I'm close to the others, but Jasper and I are nearly as close as Lucius and me.

I try not to cry when we leave the guys and head down to the car so Lucius can take me to the airport. I don't want to cry. If I'm going to cry, I want it to be when I say goodbye to the man I love.

We're quiet on the drive, the only sound the GPS barking out directions. When he parks the car, he again helps me with my bags. I check my two duffel bags and my notebook and cameras are in my backpack, which counts as my carry on.

We walk toward the security gate. Since I've already checked in I don't have to go through security right away, so we find a spot close by where we can be out of everyone's way. Lucius holds me to him and I let him, knowing he wants to because he doesn't want me going, but will let me anyway. I'm pretty sure I know what I'm going to do, but I need to have some time away from my lust-filled brain to make sure it's what I really want. I just haven't told Lucius what it is yet.

When it's finally time for me to go through security, I lean up to kiss him. "I love you, I'll let you know when I get there."

"I love you too, baby," he replies before giving me one last passionate kiss. He holds me with one hand in my hair and the other on my ass, pressing me to him. The kiss is sure to leave my lips bruised and remind me of what I'll be missing.

Pulling away, I walk through security. Before turning the corner to head toward my gate, I give one last look back and wave. His hands are tucked in his pockets, his shoulders curled inward. The pitiful expression on his face shows how sad he is to see me leaving, and I know I'm sad to be leaving too. Seeing him like that gives me a twinge of guilt to be leaving. We knew a month was all we would have before I had to go back, unless my bosses decided they wanted more information. But I gathered more than enough to make them happy, that they didn't need anything else.

I find my gate and sit down to wait until boarding is called. I'll have to go through customs in Minneapolis since I'll be crossing the border then. My layover is just over an hour, so I should have plenty of time for that and to make my connection. Most times going through customs, I make it through quickly, thanks to my press pass that proves I work for a magazine.

I sleep for the first leg of my flight, exhausted from not getting much sleep the night before. The woman next to me tries to talk to me, but after popping on my earphones and turning on my iPod she leaves me alone.

I jerk awake, realizing that we're descending into Minneapolis. I slept practically the whole flight. I turn off my iPod and glance out the window, wondering what Luc is doing now.

Chapter Twenty-Four

LUCIUS

I HATED SAYING GOODBYE TO TONI. HAVING SPENT the past month with her was amazing. I knew I wouldn't be the only one to miss her; Jas has a soft spot for her. I know once I fall asleep she sneaks from bed to go work on social media stuff with him and they talk. I'm glad he's opening up to someone; he needs someone he can talk to. But I also know the rest of the guys will miss her too. It's been nice having someone around whom we all get along with. I'm just glad the guys like her, because I plan to keep her with me for as long as I can.

Watching her walk away from me at the airport was something I didn't enjoy. But she has a job to get back to, even though we offered her one. I know Jas wants to hire more people to handle our social media, something we refused to have our manager do because we want to pick people we trust.

As I stand watching her walk through security, turning to wave, I can't help but feel unhappy for several reasons. The biggest being the fact that she never gave me an answer to my spur of the moment proposal. It's not every day I ask a woman to marry me. Another being that I've gotten used to having her fall asleep in my arms and waking up with her still there. And I can't forget the way she makes me feel. I've been happier this past month than I've ever been.

I wanted to beg her to stay, but if I made her stay, she would eventually resent me for it. She needs time to come to terms with not only our relationship, but everything that comes with it. It's bad enough she had to deal with Nikki showing up and nearly ruining things before we even got started.

I have learned that Toni needs time to mull things over; she's always waiting for the worst to happen. From what she has shared with me of her childhood, I don't blame her. I just wish I could give her the confidence she needs to believe we can have a real relationship. I know she hasn't told me everything about her past, that there is some abuse she's been through that she doesn't want to share with me. I just hope she doesn't regret our time together.

As I make my way back to the hotel, I can't help but wonder when I'll get to see her again. We have months on the road ahead of us. Maybe during our down time I can hop a flight to go see her for a few days if she's home. Or, if she can get time off, I can fly her down to visit, even if it's just for a weekend. Any time together is better than none.

Back in the room I crash; we didn't exactly sleep much last night.

The pounding at the door wakes me. I groggily reach for Toni, only to remember she's gone. Scowling, I get up to answer the door.

My brother is waiting for me on the other side. "Time to get going. Everyone is already heading down to the bus."

"Fuck, I'll be down in a few minutes." I'm exhausted. What little sleep I did get wasn't enough. I'll just have to get some more on the bus to our next destination.

We're heading north again. Whoever planned this tour thought that going from north to south and back north was a great idea. Sure, we're hitting more cities, but it just means a long-ass time travelling. Thankfully, the next city isn't that far and the crew should have already left so they can get things set up.

I grab my bag and check my phone quickly, disappointed that there's not an update on Toni's trip home. Hopefully she's getting some much-needed sleep while she's in the air.

I make my way down to the waiting bus to find everyone else already on. Nic and Chris are already playing a game, Jas is scowling down at his tablet, and Al is watching Nic and Chris play. I head to the bedroom in the back to drop my bag. It will be weird not sleeping in there now that Toni is gone; her perfume still lingers in the air and it sends a little pang to my heart.

Fuck me. This is going to be torture having her gone. I miss her already and she's only been gone a few hours, most of which I'd been sleeping.

As I head back toward the front of the bus, I grab a beer from the fridge and flop down on the couch next to my brother. I watch the TV screen with no real interest, more lost in my own thoughts. Part of me worries that I'll lose Toni, and another part of me wants to figure out when I can see her again.

When I finish my beer, I get up to put the empty away and decide to get some more sleep. I head to the bedroom rather than my bunk, knowing it'll be quieter back there and easier for me to get some much-needed rest.

The lingering scent of Toni helps me drift to sleep, even though it makes me miss her all the more.

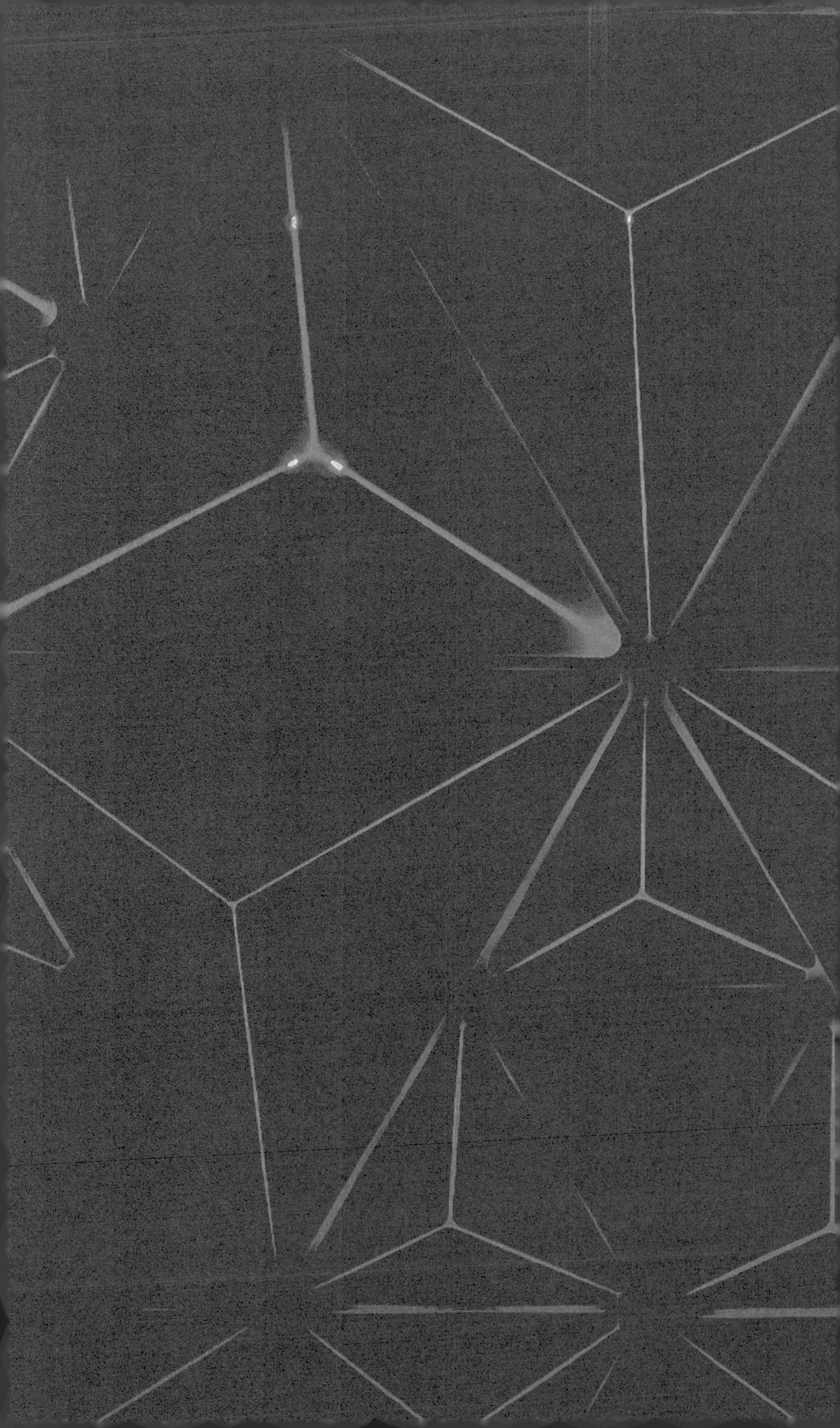

Chapter Twenty-Five

TONI

As I walk out of the gates at the airport in Edmonton, I find Keri quickly in the crowd. I walk toward her, carrying all my bags. She grabs one of my duffels and leads me out to where she's parked the car.

"You look exhausted," she says.

"Yeah, long night of saying goodbye," I reply with a grin. "Boy do I have a lot I need to catch you up on. But I first need a shower and a decent meal. The crap they served on the flight was less than appetizing."

"I have to say, I've enjoyed seeing the photo updates of you and the hottie. You look so happy in the pictures. Even the ones that fans have taken and posted. In fact, there was one uploaded this morning of a certain kiss that took place."

I can feel my eyes as they bulge out of their sockets. "There's what?" I pull my phone out and power it on for the first time since leaving Minneapolis. I immediately go searching and find the post on the band page and see that there are a ton of comments already. You can see me pressed against him, with his hand clearly on my ass while the other is fisting my hair. I look like I was clinging to him. Some of the comments range from mild to full-on hate messages about me. "Oh. My. God!"

I send Lucius a text letting him know I landed, and then ask if he's seen the photo and comments. I can't believe this is happening. A passionate kiss that was meant to be private has gone viral. I can only hope our families don't see it, but I can assume at least his will, since they're followers on the band's pages. This is going to be a PR nightmare, and I'm sure my boss won't be happy about it either.

When I don't get a reply back right away, I know he must be busy. Most likely getting ready for their show tonight. They would have left to head to the next venue some time after I caught my flight home since the roadies had left the day before to arrive on time to get things set up. "I can't believe that it's gone viral, Keri. Our families may see that."

"Toni, who cares if your family sees it? All they will see is how happy you both are, and you can't deny that he makes you happy," Keri admonishes.

Smiling, I reply, "I was happy."

"Was?"

"I'm terrified right now. I'm so glad I'm home so that I can finally talk to you and get your opinion."

She glances over at me. "Ok, talk then."

I let out a huge sigh. "Well, I've been helping Jasper with their social media a lot over the past month. Posting the pictures I've taken, answering fan questions, and that sort of thing. Anyway, Jasper wants me to stay on and keep helping them, and the rest of the guys agree that it would be a good idea. But I don't want them to get sick of me always being around; I'll have to be on tour with them."

"Seems to me like they've enjoyed your company just as you did theirs. I've seen the group selfies that were taken with you in their midst. It's obvious that they like you."

"That's just it. Lucius says the guys respect me and enjoy having me around. They treat me like one of the guys, even though I'm not."

"And?"

"Well, I love hanging out with them. It was fun to actually enjoy myself while still doing my job and helping them. But who's to say that eventually they won't get sick of me being there all the time?"

"What about Lucius?"

"He didn't want me to leave. He asked me to stay, but he wouldn't push it like he pushed for me to go on the trip in the first place. He said I needed to make the decision on my own. Part of me wanted to stay so badly, but another part of me was glad to be leaving. I was glad to be getting the space to be able to think without lust getting in the way. But at the same time, I knew I was going to miss having him sleeping next to me."

"Toni, he's right. You need to make the decision on your own. I can't tell you what to choose. I can help you sort through the pros and cons of everything, but ultimately the decision is yours."

I know she's right. So, I decided to drop the bomb. "He said he wants to marry me."

Her head whips in my direction. "He said what?"

I laugh to myself. "He said they have a few days in Vegas and he can fly me down to visit. He said while we're there we could always get married."

With Keri's eyes back on the road, she screeches, "And you left him? The man tells you he wants to marry you, which means he must love you, and you just left him?"

"What was I supposed to do, throw away my career and become a groupie who follows them around everywhere?"

"Toni, men don't just tell women they want to marry them on a whim or for shits and giggles. Men only tell women that when they love them. I highly doubt he even thought of marriage with any of his previous girlfriends."

"Keri, we're young. Deciding to get married is a big decision and commitment. We haven't even been together that long."

"Do you love him?" she asks.

Blushing a little, I answer honestly, "I do. But I feel so insecure about our relationship. He hasn't done anything to make me feel this way, I just can't help but feel like I'm not deserving of him. He's so different than his public persona. He's so kind and fun. He deserves someone who makes him happy and doesn't have the baggage I have dragging him down."

"That's a load of bull, Toni. You deserve to be happy, and if he makes you happy, then why throw it all away? I've seen the pictures posted of the two of you together, and you both look happy. You know that love has no time limit, people fall in love at first sight. Remember, you're the one who dragged me to the bar six years ago in order to be able to see him. I think you fell for him then."

"What should I do then?" I ask.

"I'd be telling our boss you quit and head back to him. I'd marry his fine ass. But that's what I would do. You have to do what you want to do, what feels right for you," she replies.

"You're not making this any easier, Keri. Maybe I should talk to mom and get her advice. You know, I'm actually closer to my family now then I have ever been."

"And I bet it's because of him."

"Yeah, it is."

"Well it's a Thursday, and I know you have to work tomorrow. You look beat. Why don't we order in, and then you can head to bed to catch up on the sleep you missed last night with your mattress gymnastics."

"Mattress gymnastics?"

"Bedroom rodeo. Boinking. Boning. Bumping uglies. Dancing in the sheets. Take your pick." She laughs.

"Keri, I don't want to know where you came up with some of those euphemisms," I say with a laugh.

She pulls into her parking spot and we drag my stuff up to our apartment. "I'm going for a shower while you order in something."

As I grab my toiletry bag and head to the bathroom, my phone dings with a message.

Luc: *I saw the post. I'm not ashamed to let people see that I love you. I hope you aren't.*

Me: *What will your family think when they see that?*

Luc: *As long as there's no sex, they won't care.*

Are you really that upset over it?

Me: *Don't you feel like our privacy has been invaded?*

Luc: *Baby, it comes with the territory. It happens.*

Me: *Have you not seen some of the comments that people left?*

Luc: *They can write what they want. It won't change the fact that I love you.*

Me: *Do you think I'm overreacting with my response to the photo?*

Luc: *You've never been exposed to anything like this before. It takes some getting used to. I just don't want you to get hurt by it. But there is nothing I can do to stop fans from taking pictures when we're out.*

Me: *I love you. Thank you for being patient with me.*

Luc: *I can't wait to see you again. Hopefully it's soon. I'm gonna miss you sleeping in my arms.*

Me: *I'm gonna miss sleeping in your arms too. I'm heading to my parents' tomorrow, so I'm not sure how much time I'll have to talk. Maybe Mom can give me some advice. ;)*

Luc: *I'll try to call you after the show, will text you first.*

Me: *Ok. if I don't reply it could be cuz I'm asleep*

already. I'm exhausted from your insatiable appetite.

Luc: *If I don't talk to you tonight, sleep well, baby. I miss you already.*

Me: *I miss you too.*

I shower and change into my normal sleep attire of shorts and tank top so that I'll be ready for bed after eating. Keri and I keep the conversation light while we eat; she knows I'm still pondering my decision of what to do about Luc. I know that no matter what, she will support and accept any decision I make regarding my relationship.

Completely exhausted, I fall into bed, and I'm asleep as soon as my head hits the pillows.

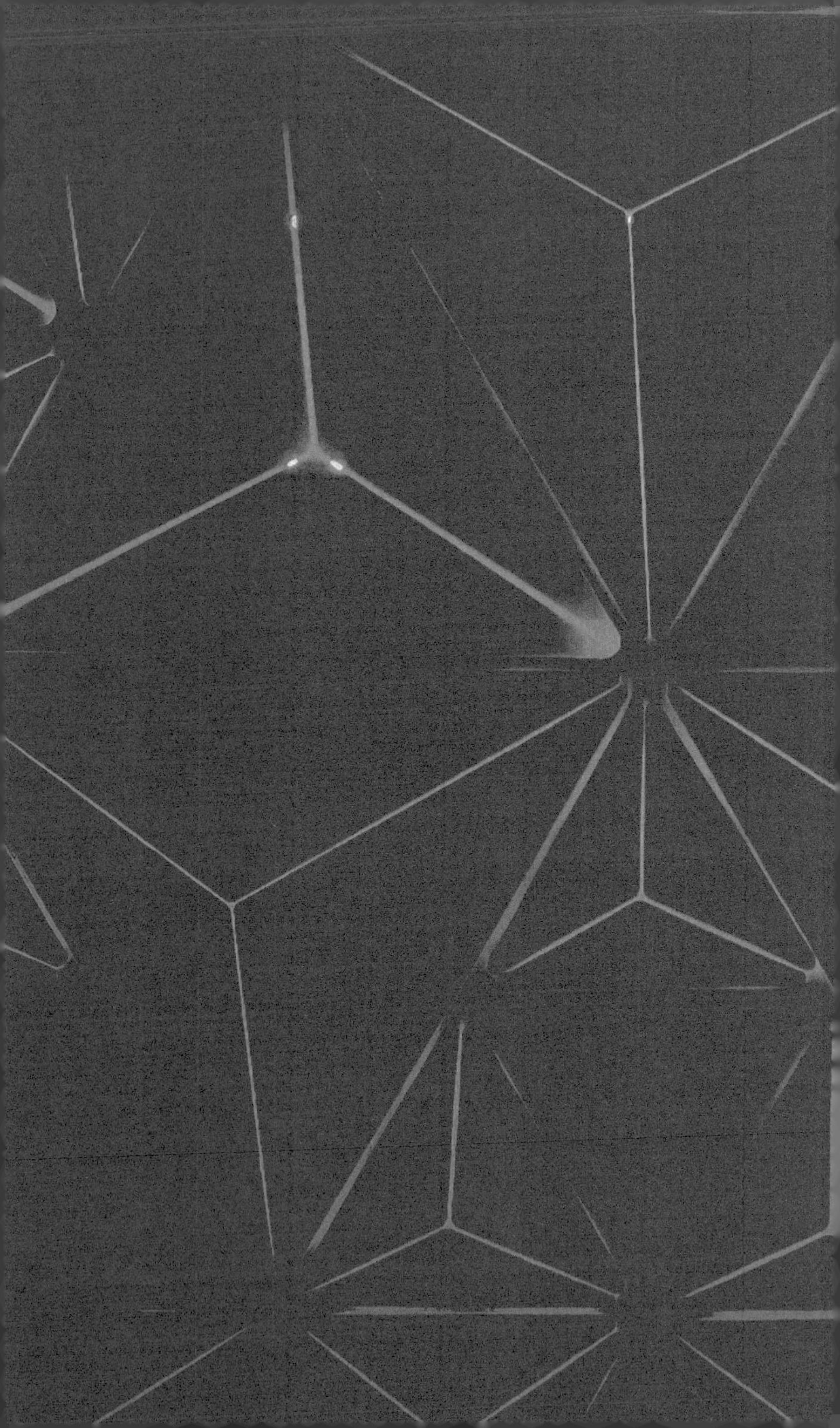

Chapter Twenty-Six

TONI

I WAKE TO MY ALARM GOING OFF. ROLLING OVER, I reach for Lucius only to feel an empty space. Opening my eyes, I realize I'm in my room, alone. I've gotten so used to snuggling into him that it's automatic to reach for him. I sigh, slightly sad that I'm not with him. I check my phone to find several texts from him.

Luc: *Hey, baby, show's over.*

Luc: *You awake?*

Luc: *Guess you fell asleep.*

Luc: *Good night, baby. Hope you have a great sleep.*

I smile to myself. I'm a little sad that I missed getting to talk to him. I get up and head to the kitchen to get coffee before I start to get ready for work. I find Keri already with the pot on and pouring us both a cup. With a sleepy smile, I say, "Morning, Keri."

"Morning, Toni. Will you be ready in half an hour?"

"Should be," I reply, as I take a sip of the coffee, carrying the cup back to my room.

Knowing that Fridays are casual, I pick out a pair of capris and a nice shirt. I pull my hair back into a ponytail and begin pulling out my notebook, tablet, cameras, and external drives, transferring them to my computer case so I can bring it to work with me. I didn't send any photos while I was on the road and have a file on the external drive for the ones I want to give my boss for the article.

On the way to work I sneak in a quick call to Luc, secretly pleased that he was already awake. Talking to him makes me miss him more. As we pull into a parking spot I quickly end the call, not before Luc can ask me to marry him again.

Getting to work, I find that my boss, Rick, is in a foul mood. Standing in his doorway, I knock to announce myself. "What," he barks without looking up.

"I'll be emailing you shortly with my full notes and some of the photos from the trip," I reply.

"Good, they're chomping at the bit to get that information so they can get the article done and ready to be published. Hopefully you kept your personal opinions out of it."

I step into his office and close the door behind me. "Since when have I been known to put my personal opinions in anything I've submitted? Sure, I'm dating one of the members of the band, but I can remain objective. My relationship status has no bearing on the quality of work I do."

"You've never been involved with subjects before," he snaps.

"Do you have a problem with me?" I ask boldly. He's almost always an asshole to me, has been from day one. But this attitude he has going on is above and beyond his normal assholishness.

"Yeah, you're a pain in my ass."

"Fine, I quit. And since my work hasn't been submitted, I'll just go have a chat with Mitch about getting my pay before I even think of passing the information along." I turn and leave. I slam the door behind me, causing a few people to look my way.

I grab my bags and head up to Mitch's office. Thankfully, Mitch isn't busy so I am shown in right away. I give him the rundown on what just happened, along with my resignation. I tell him I can't work with a man who doesn't respect someone who has worked their ass off for them for as long as I have and continually take his shit. I was done with it. He cuts me a check for my pay for the time I was gone and says I can email him the files so he can ensure they get where they need to go. He says he is sorry to lose me, but he understands why I'm choosing to leave.

I go back to my desk and pack the couple of personal belongings I have and leave. I grab a cab home rather than ask Keri for her car; she'll need it to get home later. Once at home, I quickly send my files to Mitch before deciding to pack to head to Red Deer to visit my family. By the time I'm finished packing, there is no way I will make it to the depot to catch the next bus, so I'll just have to wait for Keri to get home since she's coming with me.

Picking up my phone, I decide to send

Lucius a text.

Me: *Hey, wondering if you're free.*

Luc: *What's up, baby?*

Me: *Can I call you?*

Luc: *Give me five minutes to find someplace quieter.*

As I wait, I think about if I should tell him I quit my job or if I should hold off for a bit. Maybe I should wait to tell him until after I've visited with my family and figure out what I want to do.

After about twenty minutes of waiting I get the message I've been waiting for.

Luc: *Sorry it took so long, but I'm free now if you want to talk.*

I immediately dial his number and wait for the call to connect. "Hey, baby."

"Hey." I hope he doesn't pick up on the sadness in my tone. God, I've missed his voice, his strength when he's held me in his arms, making me feel like the most precious thing in the world.

"What's wrong? Aren't you at work?"

"My boss is being a douche. I left work early."

"It couldn't be that bad."

"The entire time I've worked with him he's always treated me like shit. And after not being around him for a month I'd forgotten how much of an asshole he can be. I'm done putting up with his BS."

"What do you want to do about it?" he asks.

"I kinda already quit," I whisper.

"You quit? Does that mean you're going to meet up with us?" He sounds hopeful, I can hear the smile in his voice.

"I know quitting is a rash decision, but I still want time to think about it. I'm still going to visit my family this weekend with Keri. Hopefully I'll figure out what I want to do soon."

"Baby, no matter what, I love you. If you want to find another job and stay there, we'll make it work. If you want to come work for us, then we'll get you down here. I know Jasper would be stoked. If it doesn't keep you as busy as you like, I'm sure he'd be happy to completely step away from it."

"I love you too, Lucius. I promise I'll let you know once I figure out what I'm doing. I just didn't expect that I'd quit my job on a whim."

"Everything happens for a reason. I just hope that reason includes me."

I smile to myself as I self consciously play with my hair. "And what would you give up for me?"

"If it meant having you, I'd give up everything."

I mentally swoon, raising my hand to my chest in hopes to stop my pounding heart. "You know I'd never ask you to."

"I know, and you know I'd never ask you to either. I'd take what I can get even if it means quick visits as often as we can."

"You're making it hard for me to resist saying 'Fuck it' and getting on a plane right now. But I promised I'd visit my family this weekend. And I thought about maybe going to visit your parents, kinda just call them up and see if your mom wants to meet me last minute."

His low chuckle comes through the phone. "I'm sure my mom would love that. But don't let what happens with her affect us. She may try to bully answers out of you, but just remember it's cuz she wants to see me happy, considering I wasn't before."

"The idea of meeting your mother actually scares the crap out of me. What if she doesn't like me or doesn't approve of me."

"Her approval means nothing to me. Her liking you or not won't affect my feelings for you. Besides, Alucard has talked to mom about us."

"OMG, I hope nothing bad."

His laughter rings through. "No, just how my attitude has changed and how happy I am."

"I'm sure you have tons of things to do, I won't keep you. But thanks for letting me call."

"Baby, I'll always make time for you, no matter what. I'm here for you. Even if it will take me some time to try to get quiet time away so I can talk to you."

"I love you, Lucius. Say hi to everyone for me."

"I will. I love you too, baby."

I end the call and sink to the couch. I didn't notice I had been pacing as I talked to Luc. Nervous energy climbed in me. Was it telling Luc that I quit my job due to my asshole of a boss or my thoughts of wanting to join the band again and take on the job they offered me? Or was it that I just wanted to be with him? All I know is that I need to figure out my shit, and fast.

I pull my notebook out and look on the band's Facebook page. The picture is still the top post and the comments are getting nastier and nastier as I read them. I can hardly believe that a bunch of catty women could be so cruel.

My Messenger window pops open with a message from Jasper.

Jas: *Sorry about the drama happening on the page. You'll like the post I'm currently writing.*

I can't help but smile to myself. Jas stepping in to help protect me from the wolves, always willing to take on the big brother role.

Me: *They're just a bunch of spiteful women jealous that they're not who he wants.*

Jas: *Posted. Hope it helps some in the future.*

Me: *I'll go check it out.*

"In light of the recent post, it has come to the band's attention that several of our page members are being abusive with some of the comments pertaining to Lucius Black's relationship with his girlfriend. As many of you know, Lucius Black had a break-up with

the ever-famous Nikki Goldburg. By chance, he ran into a woman who he'd been interested in in the past, but the timing wasn't right for them then. Lucius is currently off the market and we are happy that he has found happiness with this woman. Twisted Tragic has always been a supporter of preventing abuse and bullying, and at this time, the behaviour of several members is against what we believe in. This is the first and only warning. Anyone caught expressing this behaviour in the future will be removed and blocked from all social media accounts the band has, including personal social media. A vast majority of you owe an apology to Lucius and his girlfriend. ~ J"

Me: *OMG, Jasper, you did not just do that!*

Jas: *Lucius said the post made you uncomfortable. After reading some of the comments, it pissed us all off. They have no right to say the stuff they said about you.*

Me: *Well, they're just jealous that it isn't them that he's with. Some fans get crazy when it comes to that. Those who have boyfriends are just jealous that their boyfriends are afraid to show affection in public.*

Jas: *Regardless of the reasons, we won't put up with it. I posted it in the comments of the pictures too so people can't say they didn't see it. If we see anymore, they'll be removed from the groups. If you're on modding at all today feel free to start booting people and shoot a message with who's been booted so we can keep track.*

Me: *I'll keep an eye out for sure if I'm on.*

Jas: *Take care, and we'll talk soon.*

Me: *Thanks, Jas. I missed our nightly talk last night.*

Jas: *Well, if you hadn't fallen asleep, I'm sure I would have pestered you. I could tell by the sulk Luc had that he didn't get to talk to you.*

Me: *He was sulking?*

Jas: *Oh yeah. We gave him shit about it.*

Me: *Aww. I'll tease him about it when I talk to him next.*

Jas: *Don't make him wait too long for that, him sulking is not a fun sight.*

Me: *Well, between you and me, I might be back sooner than we expected. Depends on how this weekend goes.*

Jas: *What?!*

Me: *I'll give you more details later. I've got to*

finish packing to head to my parents' place for the weekend.

Jas: *Aww, that's cruel. Leaving a guy hanging like that.*

Me: *LMFAO. I am sure Luc would disagree with that!*

Jas: *You sure? I seem to remember something about a marriage in Vegas and no answer.*

Me: *You heard that?*

Jas: *Yeah, I was in the bathroom. I overheard you and Luc on the phone. And you just confirmed that there was no answer given.*

Me: *OMG, please tell me you didn't tell the others about that.*

Jas: *Nah, your secret is safe with me.*

Me: *Thanks, Jas. I love you!*

Jas: *Ha, wait till Luc hears that you told me you love me!*

Me: *Now I'm starting to hate you!*

Jas: *lol. I love you like a sister, Toni. Hope you know we all do.*

Me: *Jerk.*

Jas: *I got to poke fun where I can.*

Me: *Yeah, yeah.*

I roll my eyes. Of course, he'd want to poke

fun.

Jas: *Talk to you later, sweetheart.*

Me: *Ya, talk to you later, Jas.*

I turn off my notebook and head to my room to sort through my bags and pack for my weekend with my family. Practically everything I had packed for my month on tour with the guys is dirty; having an opportunity to get laundry done was a rare thing. Usually if we stayed at a hotel we would make use of their services. I toss everything into the laundry hamper, knowing I'll have to do laundry when we get back.

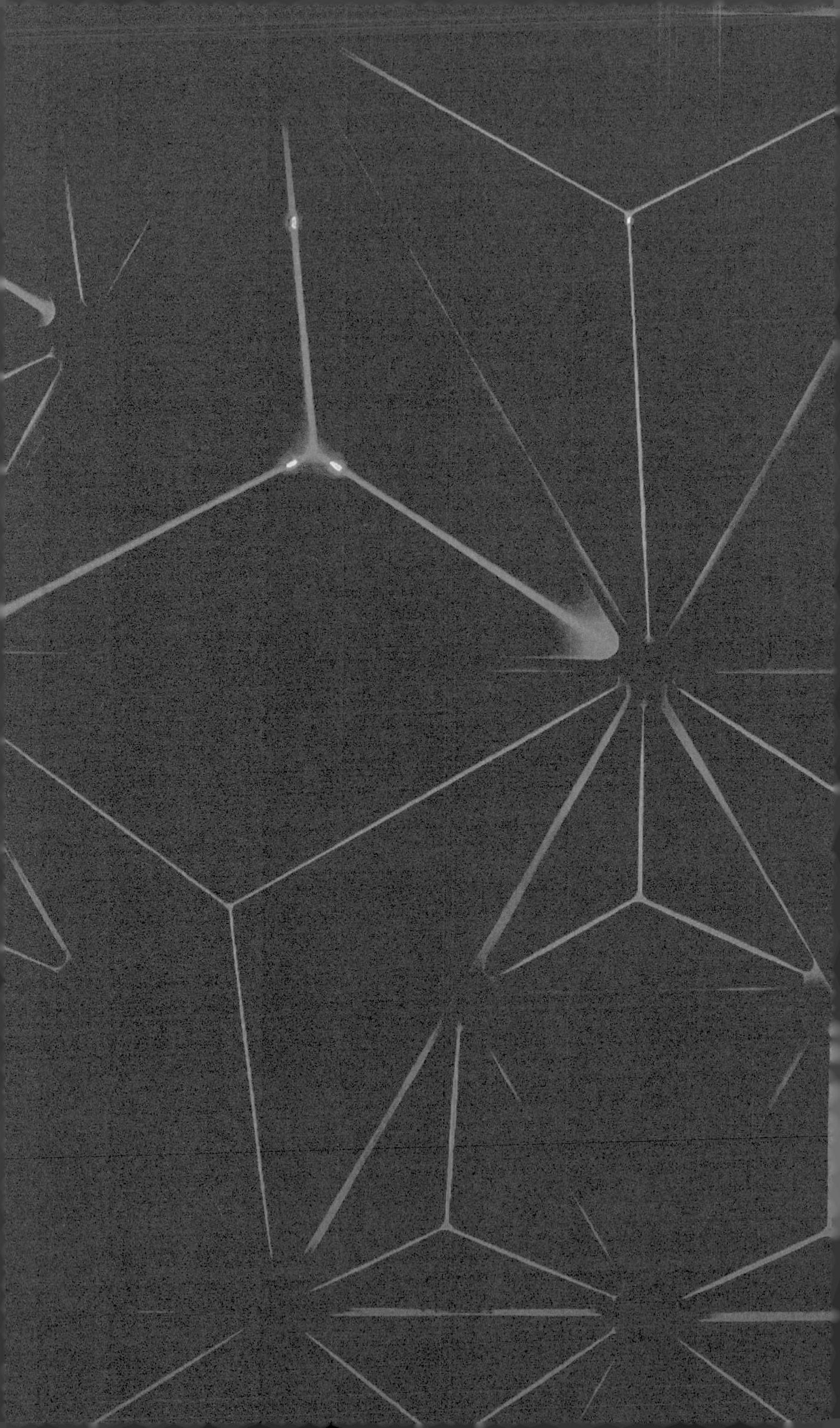

Chapter Twenty-Seven

TONI

Arriving home after my weekend with my parents, I was left feeling confused. My mom and I had gone out for a spa day with my sister, Jessica, and I talked to them about my relationship. I was pretty sure Jessica was a little envious, but she didn't show it. Mom only worried about my happiness. She told me that it's possible to love someone at first sight. Apparently, it was how it was for her and Dad. She explained that a lot of my feelings were due to my unconventional upbringing and that she hoped I could take a chance just to see where things went.

We talked a lot about my past and how it affected the way I think and feel about myself. She said she wished she could have broken down my barriers so she could have helped to change the way I thought about myself and help nurture me. I feel guilty that I tried to shut them out. I was just so used to waiting for the carpet to be pulled from under my feet, and that was my defense against getting hurt again.

What left me confused was the fact that she said she wasn't sure if I was ready for a commitment of marriage just yet, that I needed to learn to walk before I run. That if he did love me, he wouldn't try to rush me into it, and to just wait until we know we are ready. But she wasn't sure if the relationship would be healthy for me if I wasn't with him all the time; that my insecurities could ruin it. I had told her that Lucius's idea of curing my insecurities was to get married, so that I knew he was mine and I was his. I told her he had given me no reason to be insecure, that I just was.

The spa day had been wonderful. I had gotten a manicure, pedicure, full body massage, facial, and my hair done. It was a day of spoiling. I regretted that I didn't take the opportunities to bond with them and do stuff like this when I was younger.

My dad, of course, had heard of the band

and actually knew the Blacks, though our families had never met before. He said that, though he didn't want that lifestyle for his daughter, he couldn't stop me if that's what I chose. He wanted me to make mistakes so that I could learn from them, just like he wanted that for Jessica and Dean.

Overall, I didn't get the guidance I had thought I would. So, I sat in my room on Sunday night pondering what I wanted. And what I want is to be with Lucius. But I want to surprise him, make it so that he doesn't know I'm coming. But I need help with my plot, and the only person I can think of getting help from is Jasper.

I grab my cell and send Jasper a text while I boot up my computer to start looking at flights.

Me: *Hey, Jas, I need your help, but you can't tell Luc.*

Jas: *I'll text you when he's in bed. Hurry up and text him to call you, so then he can go to bed and we can talk.*

Me: *Ok, thanks!*

I quickly send Lucius a text letting him know I'm home and available to talk.

A few moments later his ringtone starts to play. Answering my phone, I say, "Hey."

"Hey."

"I miss you.

"Aww, baby, I miss you too."

"So, where are you now?"

"Nashville."

"And where to next?"

"As soon as the crew finish packing up from tonight's show we'll head to Louisville, and then on to Indianapolis after that. Thankfully in Indianapolis we'll have a few days for a break."

"So, we'll have more time that we can talk, maybe even get some sexting in."

My toes curl at the sound of his laugh coming through the speaker. "Yeah, baby, we can get some of that in, but I'd rather see pictures."

"Perv. How am I supposed to take pictures while trying to type and touch myself?"

"Oh fuck, baby. Don't tease me like that." I can hear his groan, and I know he's already picturing it. "How soon can you come visit?"

"Aww, are you suffering blue balls?"

"No, but I will be later."

I giggle. "Aww, hunny, I'm sorry."

"No, you're not."

"Nope, I'm really not. But just think how explosive it'll be next time we're together."

He chuckles. "More like over the second I get in you. But you know I can make it up to you."

"Oh yeah, I know."

"So, how was your visit?"

"It was good. I had a spa day with my mom and sister today. Keri had gone to visit her family."

"A spa day? I didn't figure you for a spa girl."

I laugh. "They're relaxing. Especially the full body massage. Too bad my sister got the better masseuse. How are the guys?"

"Those assholes. Fuck, they're annoying the crap out of me right now."

"Is it because they're teasing you about sulking?"

"Who told you I'm sulking? I'll beat his ass?"

I giggle. "I'm not telling, he's got a pretty nice ass."

The growl that comes over the line makes

me giggle even more. "You'd better be joking, baby, I don't want to have to kick their ass."

"I'm just teasing," I say while still laughing. Although, Jas does have an amazing looking ass.

"Since we have a break when we're in Indianapolis, why don't I catch a flight after the show to come see you and I can fly back to Detroit to meet up with the guys in time for the show we have there? Depending on the flights, I'd get at least a day and a half, maybe two with you."

"Don't book just yet. I'm not sure what I'm doing. My old boss's boss emailed me Friday evening, asking me to come in tomorrow to meet with him. I'm not sure what Mitch wants yet."

"I just want to see you. I miss you."

"I miss you too. But it's something we have to get used to. What happens when we start a family and you go on tour? There's no way we can bring a baby with us, and I wouldn't want a child not to have structure."

"I know, but until then I want to be selfish and keep you with me."

I can't help but smile. "Let me see how tomorrow goes. I want to know what Mitch has to say."

"Ok. Let me know how it goes, even if it's just a text. But, I'm getting pretty tired, I was trying to stay awake so I could talk to you."

"Aww, no more late nights because I'm not there?"

"No, I'm sleeping like shit because you aren't here."

"Have a good sleep. I love you, Lucius."

"Love you too, baby. Sweet dreams."

I hang up, smiling. I don't really have a meeting with my old boss, but he didn't need to know that. I just had to stall him from coming here for my plan to work.

My phone vibrates in my hand. Looking down, I see a text from Jasper.

Jas: *Want me to call?*

Me: *Are you far enough away from him that he won't be able to hear us?*

Jas: *We told his moody ass to use the bedroom, so we don't have to deal with his sulking. So, he's out of earshot.*

Me: *Ok, call.*

Seeing Jasper's face lighting up my screen, I click on accept. "Hey, Jas!"

"Hey, sweetheart. What's up?"

"I want to surprise Lucius."

"Ok?"

"Well, I quit my job Friday. I was thinking since you're heading to Louisville tomorrow, if I can get a flight in that maybe one of you can pick me up from the airport. If I can't get a flight in time, I can always meet you in Indianapolis. Even if I just fly into Indianapolis and spend a night at a hotel would be fine."

"Fuck, I have the perfect idea. Hang on a second." After what feels like forever, I hear Jasper, "Ok, sweetheart. I'm going to send you a text shortly with information for your flight. We're going to get you a room at the hotel where we'll be staying. I'm getting Al to call the hotel to make sure the room is the same one that Luc will be in."

"Devious."

"We'll text you when we're on our way up. Get packing and get to bed. Your flight is at six fifteen tomorrow morning. You'll arrive at two thirty-three p.m. local time, with a layover in

Denver for about an hour. That will give you the night to relax. I'll text you when we're at the hotel so you can surprise him."

"Thanks, Jas. Have I told you lately that I love you?"

"I know you do, sweetheart. Get ready. We'll see you soon. Don't forget to pack your gear too."

"I will. I'll see you guys as soon as Luc let's me out of the room," I reply, smiling. I know full well he won't be letting me out of the room the first day.

He hangs up and I whip into action. I tell Keri that I'm leaving in the morning and she comes to sit on my bed while I pack. I fill her in on my plans to join the guys and take the chance to see where things go.

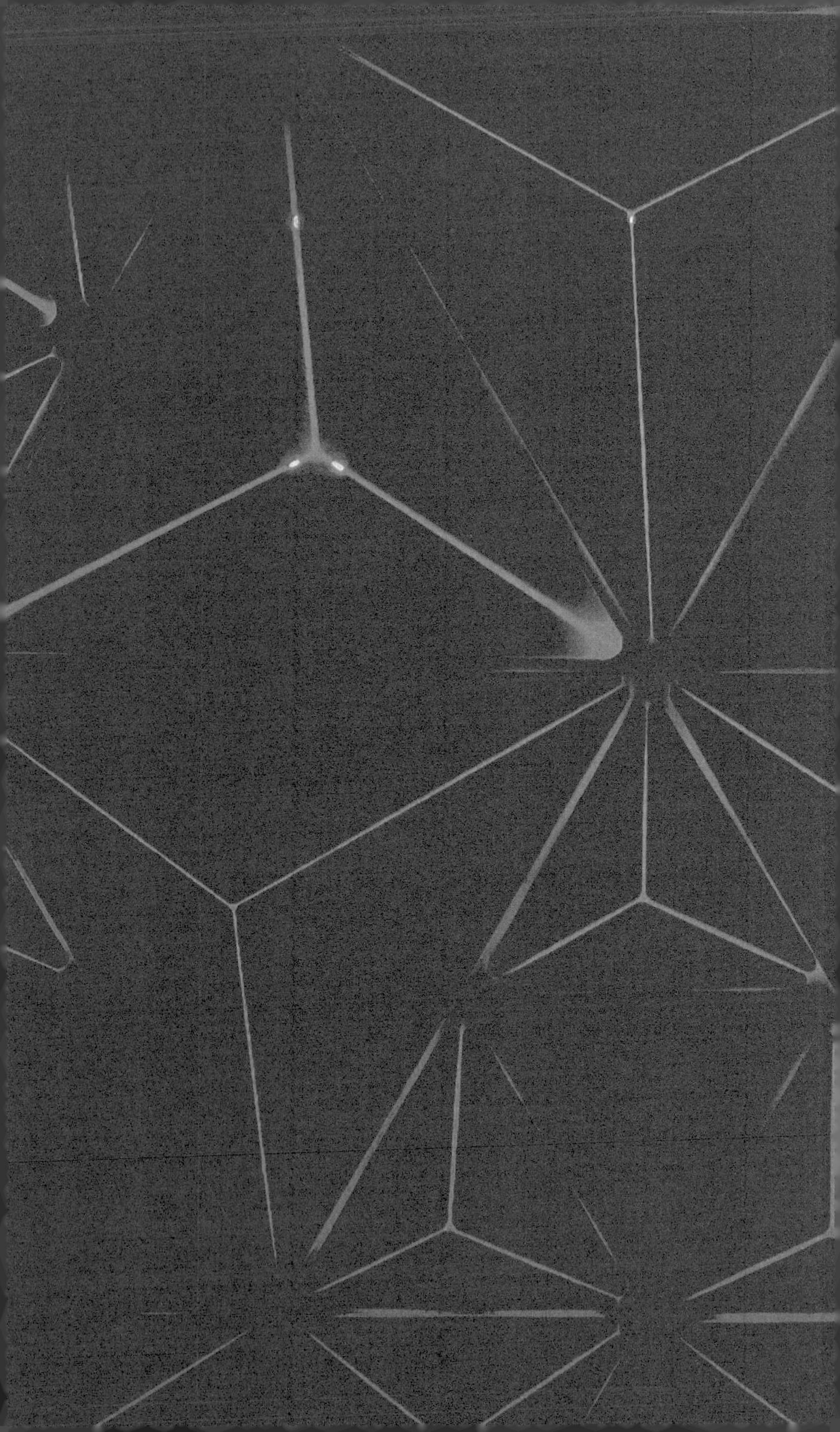

Chapter Twenty-Eight

TONI

I sit in the hotel room waiting. I know Jasper's supposed to text me when they arrive so I can be ready, but I'm nervous as all hell. I didn't talk to Lucius last night. I was too nervous that I would ruin our surprise. I slept most of the afternoon and into the night after arriving and woke early this morning in anticipation. I was excited to be able to see him again, even if it's only been a few days that we've been apart.

My phone pings with a message.

Jas: *He's got the key to the room and we're heading up.*

Me: *Ok, thanks!*

I quickly lay back in the bed to pretend I'm sleeping. Of course, once he discovers that I'm naked, I'm sure he'll be surprised and happy to see me.

My heart stops when I hear the door unlock with his key card. I try to make it look like I'm sleeping.

"What the fuck? Who the fuck let you in here?" he demands.

I let out a groan as if he's woken me and lift my head, looking in his direction. "Luc?"

"Toni?"

"Yeah."

"Fuck, baby, you scared the crap out of me. What the fuck are you doing here?"

"Surprise!"

"How long are you here for?" he asks, as he stalks toward me, stripping down to his boxers on the way.

I lick my lips, noticing his arousal. Swallowing, I rasp out "That depends."

"On?"

"How long you want me to be here?"

"Are you serious? You're going to stay?"

"Yeah. I got a one-way ticket."

Sitting on the edge of the bed, he leans down and kisses me. "Why didn't you tell me?"

"I wanted to surprise you. I had Jasper help

me plan it. Al made sure that we were in the same room. I got in town yesterday afternoon; there was no way for me to get to you yesterday in time. So we figured that surprising you here would be the best."

"Fuck, I'm glad you're here, baby."

"I know you are," I say, as I cup him.

Growling, he pushes back the covers to discover me naked. Making quick work of his boxers, he looms over me, nudging my legs open to settle between them. I pull him down for a kiss as I arch into him.

He deepens the kiss as he enters my waiting sex. We moan into each other's mouths. I know it won't take much for either of us to reach our release. We've been dancing the fine line of teasing since I left.

He's being tender, showing more restraint than I thought he would. I figured he would have ravished me and made up for it the next time. I know today we won't be leaving our room except for their show tonight.

As I lie in his arms, sated, I ask, "Good surprise?"

"Yeah, baby, it's definitely a good surprise."

"I talked with my mom some to get her opinion and perspective on some things. I do want to be with you, Luc, but I think it's too soon for us to be thinking about getting married, especially in Vegas. I think we should wait a while and see where this goes and get to know one another better before we take that step. Maybe live with one another, like a normal couple, to see if we're compatible. Sure, it's fun while on tour, but who's to say being alone twenty-four seven without the guys won't make us go crazy."

"I get it, baby. I might have jumped the gun, but I know there's no one else for me. You're it."

Leaning up, I give him a quick kiss before settling beside him with my head on his chest. Content that he knows that I want to wait, I start to drift off.

Chapter Twenty-Nine

TONI

I'M WOKEN UP BY POUNDING ON THE DOOR. LUC groans next to me. Getting up, he pulls on his boxers while I pull on the shorts and tank top that I discarded last night while waiting for them to arrive. Looking back at me before opening the door to make sure I'm decent, Luc opens the door.

I smile at the sight of Al, Jasper, Nic, and Chris grinning at me. "Hey, guys."

Jasper is the first to pull me in for a hug before I'm passed amongst them, laughing each time. "Wow, you guys miss me or something?" I ask.

Al chuckles. "Fuck no. We're glad you're back so my brother can stop sulking."

We all laugh at the same time as Luc says, "Fuck you, Al."

"Nah, that's her job. Maybe now she can get your panties out of a twist."

I can't help but snort as I laugh, which makes me laugh harder. "Oh my God, I've missed you guys," I say, as I wipe the tears from my eyes.

"Get ready, we're taking you to lunch," orders Nic.

"Um, do I have time to shower?" I ask.

"You will later, we're starving. Hurry up. We'll meet you down in the lobby. And don't get sidetracked, please."

They leave us alone to get ready. I can't help but laugh. It's not just Luc that makes me happy but the fun of antagonizing each other too. How it's so easy for us to get along. How they feel like family to me. It's ironic that they mean more to me than the family I was adopted into, and yet he's made it possible for me to become closer to my family.

As I pull on a pair of matching lace lingerie, I watch Luc out of the corner of my eye. The tenting of his black boxer briefs shows his desire for me, but as ordered, we don't have time for it. But I know once we are free of the others he's going to devour me. I'm sure all the pent-up sexual frustration was not expelled this morning when he found me naked in bed, and I know I am not nearly close to my fill of him.

I slip on a pair of hip hugger jeans and a comfortable, form-fitting tank top before sliding my feet into a pair of flip flops. I head to the bathroom to sort out some makeup and my hair. Even though I'm wearing clothes for comfort, I still want to at least look good for my man. Us girls have to look nice when going out, especially in public with the chance of us getting caught in pictures.

When I leave the bathroom ready to head out, I find Luc leaning against the window frame staring out at the world surrounding us. I drink in the sight of him. Loving how the jeans he's wearing showcase his long legs, hug the curve of his ass that I love so much, and knowing it will show some of his endowment from a front view. The t-shirt looks like it's painted on with how it's hugging his upper body. His raven hair is shorter than it was before; he's cut it since I've last seen him. I'll miss grabbing the long locks while his face is buried between my legs or when I pull on it just before I bite his neck as

I come.

As if sensing me watching him, he turns to look toward me. His blue eyes brighten from the dark color they were, almost as if he had been thinking about something bad. I can't help the natural smile that appears any time he's around me.

Taking my hand, we head out of our room to join the guys before they come looking for us--even if I'd rather be pushing him on the bed and having my wicked way with him. It'll just have to wait till later.

In the lobby, Jasper wraps his arm around my shoulder and pulls me against him. "Come on, sweetheart, let's show you how a real man should be treating his woman by showing you off rather than keeping you hidden," he teases.

I can't help the giggle that escapes. "He's a real man where it counts. Needless to say, I'm very satisfied in that department." I know I'm blushing at the reference of our sex life. Leaning my head close to his I whisper, "Thanks again for this, Jas."

I pull away from Jas so I can wrap my arm around Luc's waist and be anchored to his side.

I know some may think our constant contact is crazy and that we're insecure, but it's not that, it soothes us both. We feel whole, rather than like a half missing its matching piece. When I look up at Luc, knowing how confident he is, I never would have thought that he felt the way he did with his family; that he felt like he came second to his twin or pitied by his other brothers, despite being close to them. Who knew that two misfits like us would be perfect for one another?

We make our way to the cars that were arranged for us during our stay. But unlike vehicles we've had before, this time we have shiny black Escalades with tinted windows waiting for us. And of course, drivers to take us wherever we want to go. This could have its advantages.

Lunch is loud and boisterous. I can't help but be sucked into the playfulness they exude. I've missed hanging out with them, even if it's only been a few days since I was last with them. Although Luc would rather keep me to himself, he knows I need the socialization of others. The only thing missing is another girl for girl talk, considering Keri and I won't be able to talk much.

"So, my sister Jade wants to come out and spend the summer with us. Something about my parents and her roommates going away, and her being stuck at home alone sucking," announces Jasper.

I listen as the guys groan about having another woman around. I can't help but smile, knowing it will drive them nuts having to compete for the bathroom and having to be more modest than they are. In my month on tour with them we dropped the modesty like Al figured would happen. They've seen me naked in the bathroom and I've caught them naked. I don't blush anymore when it happens, and Luc is totally ok with me catching glimpses since he knows my relationship with his band mates is purely platonic. I think the dropping of the modesty is where the turning point was for me becoming one of them.

Feeling Luc's hand tighten on my shoulder where his arm is wrapped around the back of my chair, I look toward him. "What's that smile for, baby?"

I love how he calls me baby, but I wish he'd

have a more unique pet name for me. "Just thinking how much you would hate having another woman around, cramping your style. I'll miss getting to see five hot guys naked all the time. But then again, only one naked guy matters, and I'll get to see that regardless."

"Fuck," he curses under his breath. "Am I gonna have to tell them to start closing the door to the bathroom?"

I give him a devilish grin. "Nope. There's only one hot, naked body that does it for me. The rest are just eye candy."

Leaning over to kiss me, he mutters, "Thank Christ."

I pull away, blushing, still not used to public displays of affection, to find the guys grinning at us. "You know when each of you fall, we're going to tease you relentlessly."

"Like that'll ever happen, Toni," says Nicholai. "We're a bunch of playboys who enjoy the single life." Glancing at Luc, he adds, "Well, at least some of us were playboys."

I giggle. "Mark my words, Nic, your time is coming. And I'm going to laugh my ass off when you come to tell us that you've got your knickers in a twist over a woman. If I'm betting anything, Chris is the next to fall."

"Me? What the fuck, Toni," Christoph sputters. "Here I thought you liked me."

"You know I love you, Chris, but I have a feeling you're next, and it's going to be sooner than anyone expects," I reply sweetly, smiling at him.

"Fuck," he mutters, pouting while the rest of us laugh.

"Well, if I get any say it would be nice to have a girl around to talk to. As much as I love you all, sometimes a girl needs another girl. Sometimes we need some estrogen to level out all the testosterone."

"Are we really debating my sister joining us and cramping my style?" asks Jasper.

Al glances between me, Luc, and Jasper before saying, "You know the saying 'a happy wife, a happy life'. If we are gonna survive being happy, then Toni's right, she needs a little girl time. Besides, our tour is over in July, which means it would only be for a month."

Jasper groans. "I love you, sweetheart, but don't make us regret this. My sister can drive anyone up the wall."

I laugh. "Gee, I wonder where she gets that from."

As we sit laughing and talking, a couple of fans come over to our table and ask for an autograph. They're beautiful girls, and I admit I was surprised that Luc kept his focus on me rather than paying them any attention, other than giving them an autograph. That's just one example of what I mean, that he doesn't give me reasons to be insecure with our relationship.

Nic clears his throat. "Um, if we don›t get a move on or we›re going to be late for soundcheck."

"Oh shit," I say. "I need to run back to the hotel for my camera and my pass."

"You don't need them," replies Al. "Today you can relax and just hang out."

"If I'm going to do my job, I do," I reply. "Y'all did want me handling social media for you. And you've been slacking with the crowd pictures before the show starts for the fans to tag themselves in." I can't help but laugh at the glare Jas is giving me; I totally had the opening to poke more fun at him and couldn't pass it up. If I had to admit it, I could very easily fall in love with Jasper if I didn't already love Luc. I just hope Luc never feels threatened by my friendship with Jas if he ever finds out about our past.

"Ok, let's hurry up," Al snaps.

Leaning closer to Luc, I say, "I think your brother has his panties twisted too tight around his balls. That, or he really needs to get laid."

Luc's answering laugh earns a glare from Al as he says, "I heard that, Toni."

Giggling, I let Luc lead me toward the waiting SUVs. He gives me a toe-curling kiss before opening the door for me to get in first. Knowing that he's just as turned on as I am, I hope we can have a quick fuck before they have to do the soundcheck.

In our room while the guys are waiting for us, I find myself pressed up against the wall with Luc grinding his hips into mine while kissing me hard. Moaning into his mouth I reach for his belt, but he stops my hands. "Fuck, baby, we don't have time for this, but I want you so badly."

"Then fuck me," I say, panting.

Groaning, he lifts me and carries me to the bed. Placing me on my feet, he peels my pants down part way before shoving his down enough to free himself. He turns me around and bends me over the bed before thrusting into me.

"Fuck," I pant.

As if he has no control, he powers into me over and over, making quick work of sending us over the edge. It's hard and fast, just how I want it. He's showing my body who owns the pleasure it brings by being with him. I can feel myself tightening around him. My body so close to release, but holding back from slipping over the edge, wanting it to last longer than the quick fuck we're allowing ourselves despite the others waiting for us.

"Baby, come. I'm so close with you milking me that way," his voice is laced in a deep husky tone.

That pushes me over the edge. My hands fist the comforter as I let out a scream, coming hard. Even lost in my ecstasy, I can feel it as he swells just before finding his own release, slowly rubbing out his orgasm.

We make quick work of fixing ourselves

before grabbing my stuff. Giving me a wolfish grin, I know he won't care if the other guys are pissed that we fucked, since it was quick.

Sliding next to Al in the SUV, I can't help but laugh as he groans. "Really, Luc, you couldn't wait just a few more hours before fucking?"

I blush. He must have been able to smell the sex on me. I won't be ashamed of the fact that I love his brother or that we make love. Al should know the fine line that his brother's been on during my absence and how much he's wanted to be buried inside me. And it's not like we have to answer them.

"Al, you really need to get laid to take the stick out of your ass," I snap.

"I'm sorry, Toni, but since we're supposed to be doing soundcheck now, so that things can run smoothly for tonight, my brother should be keeping things in perspective," he snaps back.

"Really, Al, you're going to go back to acting like the asshole you were to me when Luc and I first hooked up? Fuck this shit. I thought I was fitting in." Facing the driver, I demand, "Stop the fucking car, I'm going back to the hotel."

"Baby, don't," Luc says, as he gently

squeezes my leg.

"Out of my way," I snap at him.

Luc glares at Al. "Way to go, brother. You've pissed her off, and now I can't stay to calm her down," he says, as he opens the door to let me out. I know he's torn between wanting to stay with me and having to do their soundcheck.

"I'm booking a ticket home for your last day here. I sure ain't sticking around if he's going to be an asshole," I say softly, my voice still thick with anger, fury coursing through my veins.

"Baby, don't. We'll talk about this when I get back. We'll be back after the soundcheck, and we'll order some room service so we can talk. Don't leave," he says before giving me a quick kiss.

The look of longing he gives me before getting back in the SUV is nearly my undoing, but I stiffen my spine and turn to head back to the hotel. I don't have to put up with Al being pissed at me, especially for no reason. And I sure as hell am not going to get in between brothers. Al can kiss my ass if he ever thinks I plan to be around him again.

Chapter Thirty
TONI

A KNOCK SOUNDS AT THE DOOR. MY BROWS furrow together. Luc wouldn't knock and I'm not expecting anyone. I sigh, rolling my eyes as I head to the door. Opening it, I find Al standing there. "What the fuck do you want?" I snap, still angry at him.

"Can I come in?" he asks politely. His ice blue eyes are full of an emotion that looks like regret.

"Where's Luc?" I demand, as I look beyond him for Luc.

"He's with the others. I told him I wanted to talk to you privately, to apologize," he says.

I sigh again and hold the room door open. I've changed into sweats and a tank top, figuring that I'll be staying in this evening because I was pissed off and nothing will put me in a good mood at this point, probably not even Luc. I've spent the last few hours stewing in my anger.

I slam the door closed as if to announce that I'm still angry if he didn't get it from the way I acknowledged his arrival. "Ok, so talk," I say, as I cross my arms over my chest.

"I'm sorry, Toni. I had no right to snap at you."

"Why did you?"

"Because I'm jealous."

"You're jealous?" I ask, my expression contorting in confusion.

"Yeah. I'm lusting after my brother's girlfriend and knowing he just fucked you when I want nothing more than to do the same thing isn't sitting well. Sure, I knew he wanted you six years ago, but it doesn't stop me from wanting you too."

I swallow. "Ok, I'm confused. How does that relate to when you were pissed with me in Edmonton?"

"Because I wanted you then too. But because my brother was happy, I put aside how I was feeling. But when you left, I'd gotten used to not having you near me, tempting me.

Then, knowing you were coming back, I tried to brace myself for the jealousy to eat me alive. But smelling the sex on you when you got back in the SUV pushed me over the edge, because I wanted you."

I'm shocked. The dark and dangerous brother wants me. Six years ago, he could have had me, but it wouldn't have taken long for me to figure out that it was his brother I really wanted. "Does Luc know?" I ask, fearing that his brother may know of his desire for me. Something that may piss off Luc if he knew.

"No, I spun off some BS that I was jealous I wasn't getting any."

"Al, I love you, but not the way I love Luc. I love you like a brother," I say, as I look away, feeling sad for him. I can only imagine how tough it is for him to want what his brother has.

His long legs eat the distance between us, and his knuckle turns my chin up to look at him. "I'm not telling you this to make you feel pity for me. I'm telling you this because you deserve to know that I want you."

Tears stream down my cheeks. "Al, you can't. It's wrong. It'll only hurt your brother, and I won't come between you."

He wipes away my tears in an uncharacteristic act of tenderness. "I promise that Luc will never know about how I feel about you, at least not from me. And I know he'll kick my ass, and I would deserve it. And if he's going to kick my ass, then I might as well make it worthwhile." He dips his head toward me and I try to back up only to collide with the wall. His hands are braced on both sides of me, effectively penning me in. He takes my mouth in a hot, wet kiss.

Shocked, I gasp, and he takes full advantage by slipping his tongue in. My hands move up to his chest and I shove him back. He lets me. I slap his face. "How dare you. Get out," I yell.

He leaves the room without saying anything. I don't even notice I'm crying again until I taste the salt on my lips. I sink to the floor and wrap my arms around my legs as I begin to sob. Luc is going to be pissed at me; he'll never forgive me for this. He's going to want to kick his brother's ass. This could ruin the rest of their tour, all because of me.

Feeling suddenly dirty, I head to the bathroom and turn the shower on to the hottest it will go. I step into the scalding stream after stripping down and let the hot water flow across my skin before I start to scrub my body through my blurred vision.

"Toni," Luc calls out. He sounds concerned. I can tell it's Luc because his voice always softens when he talks to me, with others his tone can come across as harsh at times.

Hearing him calling out, sounding concerned about me, makes me feel even worse. I sink to the floor of the shower and continue to sob. I let his brother kiss me without stopping it, other than backing away. I should have pushed him away then, instead of gasping and allowing him to try to coax me into the kiss. I should never have been in this situation; I should never have come. I should have stayed home and tried to find a new job.

I can feel him watching me through the glass shower doors. I can't bring myself to look at him, completely ashamed of myself. I'm a fucking harlot. First, I slept with one of his best friends and now I've kissed his brother, his fucking brother. I don't deserve to be with him, he deserves someone better than me.

I hear the shower door open and the clunk of boots before I feel him pulling me into his arms. I can feel the roughness of his jeans against my legs. He cradles me to his chest. "Baby, what's wrong?"

He doesn't know why I'm upset. He doesn't know how to deal with crying women. He won't know how to deal with the woman he loves having kissed his brother or fucked his friend. I cry even more at his tenderness, his one hand rubbing up and down my arm, trying to comfort me, while the other is cradling my head to him. I don't deserve his comfort.

He holds me until the water runs cold and I'm shivering. The tears have stopped and I'm hiccupping. I know my face will be blotchy and snotty, and my eyes will be bloodshot and swollen. Adjusting his hold on me, he shifts to turn the water off before standing with me in his arms. Setting me on the counter, he wraps a towel around me before stripping his soaked clothes and drying himself off. Then he focuses on drying me off.

I don't deserve him being tender to me. I don't deserve to have him taking care of me right now. I deserve him to scream at me, to tell me to get lost.

When both my body and hair are dried, he carries me into the bedroom and settles on the bed, shifting us so that I'm laying in his arms, but we're on our sides facing one another. His legs tangle with mine, holding me to him.

"What's wrong, baby?" he asks quietly, as he tips my face to his. I cast my eyes down, not sure if I can look at him. "Baby, look at me."

I look up at him and my vision blurs with fresh tears from the concern and pain I see in his eyes. It's hurting him to see me like this and not knowing how to fix it. Swallowing and taking a deep breath, I try to tell him, but nothing comes out. I can't tell him something that will hurt him.

"Baby, please tell me what's got you so upset," he demands softly. "I hate seeing you like this. Let me fix it."

"You can't fix it," I finally whisper before burying my head in his chest.

"Is this about Al?" he asks.

Knowing I can't talk without betraying the emotions that are battling within me, I nod. The love I have for this man and the self-loathing I have for myself are tearing me apart.

"Did he come to apologize?"

I nod again. Finally realizing that I need to stop hiding and tell him the truth, I look up at him. "Oh, he apologized. Then told me he wanted to fuck me. He trapped me against the wall and kissed me. I gasped in shock, so he took advantage and thrust his tongue in my mouth. When I got over the shock, I pushed him away from me and slapped him before telling him to get out." I felt him tense up. "I'm sorry, Lucius. I didn't expect that to happen. I don't want to come between you and your brother. You don't deserve to have someone treat you like this, you deserve so much better."

"Baby, stop with the self-loathing you're feeling. You did nothing wrong. My brother should have told me how he felt long before it came to this. Even him telling me wouldn't change how I feel about you, but it may have helped with trying to figure out how to resolve the situation rather than burying it in the sand. He never should have kissed you knowing you're mine. That's on him, not you."

Completely taken aback, I ask, "You're not

mad at me?"

"No, baby, I'm not mad at you. But I am pissed at my brother. And if you didn't need me right now, I'd be going to kick his ass. But you need me and that's more important," he says.

"How can you not be mad that I kissed your brother?"

"You didn't kiss him, he kissed you. There's a difference."

"But I didn't stop it."

"You did. Just because you didn't stop it right away because you were surprised doesn't mean that you didn't stop it. You didn't expect him to kiss you."

I take a deep breath and prepare to tell him the one thing that could break us. "There's one more thing I need to tell you, Luc. It's been eating at me for keeping it from you."

"What is it, baby?"

"I slept with Jas," I say softly.

"You what?" he roars, causing me to flinch.

"It happened a long time ago. At a party we both went to a year before I first saw you playing at the bar. Keri took me out to celebrate my seventeenth birthday. Jas and I were both drunk, and Keri had been hounding me all night to pick up a guy so I could get laid. I felt out of place because I didn't know anyone, and Jas was sitting by himself, so I approached him. I came on to him and asked him to fuck me after talking to him for a bit."

"Is there anything going on between the two of you now?" he asks, sounding almost hurt. "I know the two of you spend time together when everyone else is sleeping."

"There's nothing going on. We talked about it one night, but he doesn't remember it happening. Me being honest and talking to him about it is part of what started our friendship. He appreciated my honesty and that I wanted to clear the air so things wouldn't be awkward between us. I wanted to tell you, I just didn't know how to," I sob.

"So, you want me to believe there's nothing going on between the two of you?"

"There's nothing between Jas and me but friendship. He's like a brother to me, just like I'm like a sister to him. You can ask him for yourself." I'm panicking. He doesn't believe me.

The secret I've been terrified would pull

us apart is doing just that. He'll never trust me with Jas and will always wonder if anything is happening between us. I start sobbing again, my heart slowly cracking because I'm losing him. I start to pull away from him, needing to get out of here. But he surprises me by holding me tighter to him. "If you say nothing is going on between the two of you, then I believe you. Jas isn't the type to fuck around, and I know things back then were hard for him. If he was drunk it was probably because it had to do with the anniversary of losing Isabelle. It's the only time he allowed himself to get hammered back then."

I surge forward, hugging myself to him. Oh my God, how did I end up with someone so kind, understanding, and forgiving? He should be disgusted with me and pushing me away. He should be sending me home on the first flight available. He should not be comforting me. He should be kicking his brother's ass for even coming on to me, be pissed at me for what happened. But he's treating me like I'm a victim, not someone who was in the wrong for what happened with his brother, and to be so accepting of my history with Jas. "Why do you have to be so kind?" I ask.

"Baby, you did nothing wrong. Stop beating yourself up over it. What happened between you and Jas is in the past. I'm glad you told me, but you should have told me sooner. Any anger I have right now is toward my brother, not you," he says, as he leans in to kiss me. The kiss is so soft and gentle, his mouth coaxing mine.

I surrender to him. Pour myself into the kiss, letting him know I'm sorry, even if he doesn't think I have a reason to be. Letting him know that I really do love him.

"Why don't you order up some room service while I'm gone. I gotta go shortly, so I don't have time to eat with you. I'll grab something when I get back. Get some rest and we'll talk more later, ok?" he asks.

"You don't want me to go with you?" I ask, feeling hurt.

"I don't want you to see what I plan to do to my brother," he replies.

"Be easy on him, don't let me come between the two of you," I say pleadingly.

"Baby, he had no right to touch what is mine.

Sure, we grew up sharing everything, but that does not mean I'm willing to share my woman with him. Even if you wanted him, I wouldn't allow it."

"Maybe it will be easier if I go home after your break. I don't want things to be awkward for the tour."

He kisses me lightly. "Baby, it's already going to be awkward. I might be able to forgive Al in time, but right now I can't." He pulls away from me and starts to get dressed.

I suddenly feel cold without him and slip below the covers. My eyes start to drift closed of their own accord before Luc even leaves. I feel him kiss my forehead, telling me to rest and eat, before I hear the door close.

Chapter Thirty-One

LUCIUS

I WAS SIMMERING WITH RAGE. I HATE THAT I HAVE to leave Toni in our room in her emotional state, but we have a show to play. I wanted to stay and comfort her so badly. Not only did she shock me by telling me what my brother did, but what shocks me even more is that she slept with a guy I consider a brother. I can't even believe that they kept it from me; that kinda hurts. But even knowing that fact doesn't change the way I feel about her. I just have to take care of the real problem: my brother.

I know confronting my brother before the show will only cause a problem, so I bide my time, waiting for the show to end. Of all the things my brother could do to hurt me, this one is by far the worst. Sure, he's hit on and slept with my girlfriends before, but they never really meant as much to me as she does. Knowing how I feel about Toni, he just had to make a play for her. He had to make her want to leave just after I got her back, all because he hit on her and made her feel guilty for not only that but keeping her past with Jas from me.

What makes it worse is that as teens, Al always tried to steal my girlfriends. I thought he grew out of it when he finally had his own serious relationships. I can't remember how many girls I broke up with because they cheated on me with him. Excuses ranging from I didn't know it was him to you're just too nice. Out of the two of us, my brother was always the asshole girls flocked to.

I do my best to keep my cool while we play, but the guys can tell something is up. Our normal showmanship is lacking; my rage preventing me from feeling the high I normally get while playing. My own playing is a little off; edgy or even angry sounding. It's like I'm playing on autopilot.

As soon as the show ends, I hand off my guitar and stalk toward an empty corridor. I know Al will follow wanting to know what's up, even if he probably knows that Toni would have told me what happened. He should have told me the truth rather than just saying she was upset when he came back down from apologizing to her. But he didn't want to cause a scene, because I would have decked him then and there.

As soon as I round the corner, I can feel Alucard getting close to me; we've always been able to feel when the other is close and have even shared our emotions at times. Once he rounds the corner, I whip around, glaring at him. Ready to kick the shit out of him. Needing him as the outlet to take out my anger on for what he did.

"What the fuck happened out there? You weren't playing like you normally do," he spits.

"You know what the fuck happened out there! You fucking asshole!" I roar, lunging for him. I crash into him, sending him slamming into the wall behind him. My fist connects with his rib while I have him pinned.

Al shoves me back before landing a punch, hitting me in the chest. I swing back with a right hook, nailing him in the jaw. He hooks me in an arm lock and takes a shot at me; I take a jab at his side before shoving him off me.

"Why the fuck did you do it?" I demand. I know that my demand will go unanswered. He'll just spin me some bullshit like always. The only difference is that this is about Toni and not the other girls that I didn't give a shit about. I didn't love them like I do her.

"Because I could," he says cockily, all the while smirking at me.

"You know what she means to me, you asshole," I say, as I charge him again. "I had to leave her in the room alone. She's a fucking mess because of you."

This time we don't let up. Al deserves every ounce of anger that pours out of me as we fight. If Toni leaves me because of what he did, I don't think I'll be able to forgive him. He's fighting me back, which only pisses me off further. He gets in a few good jabs, but with my anger I'm hitting him more often.

"Why the fuck did you do it?" I demand again through breathless gasps while we spar. "You always have to try and ruin shit for me."

He grunts as my fist connects to a floating rib. We're pulled apart by Chris, Nic, and Jas. It takes both Chris and Nic to hold me back while Jas pins Al to the wall.

"What the fuck guys, why are you fighting?" Nic asks, looking back and forth between us.

"Why don't you ask Al?" I say angrily, trying unsuccessfully to shake them off.

"Dude, calm down, Luc," Chris barks, as his grip on me tightens.

My head turns toward him. "You want me to calm down after I had to leave Toni an emotional wreck because of that asshole?"

Jas looks at Al. "What the fuck did you do to Toni?" he demands.

With a cocky grin, my brother says, "I made a pass at her."

I smirk as Jas wipes the grin off Al's face with a punch. I knew Jasper had a soft spot for Toni, and him decking my brother only proves it, but it also makes me wonder if there is potentially more to their friendship due to their past. But I also know that Jas would help protect Toni from anything, including my jerk of a brother.

"Really, Alucard? You went up to apologize for being an asshole and you pull an even bigger dick move," Jas says. "Why the hell would you do that to your brother? We're not fucking teenagers anymore."

Alucard goes to shove Jas off him, but Jas doesn't back off, having expected Al to try to get loose. My brother glares at Jasper. "Like you can't deny your late-night encounters with her."

"We fucking work and talk, asshole. Don't be trying to deflect what you did on to my friendship with her. I may have a history with her, but that doesn't mean I'd cross the line you did!" Jas replies, his tone laced with anger. "I'd never do something that would jeopardize any of us."

Alucard finally manages to shove Jas off him and stalks off. Nic and Chris let go of their hold on me, Nic taking off after my brother.

"She told me," I say, looking right at Jas.

"It happened a long time ago, and I don't remember any of it," Jas replies, looking pained. "We're just friends."

"I know, man," I say. "Toni would have said something. She should have told me sooner about the two of you, but I get why she held back. She didn't want me to not trust either of you. But I see the way the two of you are together, and I know there's nothing but friendship there."

Jas grins. "She's a hell of a woman and you're lucky to have her. She's been through a lot and I'd love to kick your brother's ass for what he just did. I know she loves you; we've talked about it. Your brother just doesn't understand what she's been through and how it affects her emotionally and mentally. You're going to have to reassure her that nothing changes how you feel about her."

"I know, Jas," I say before I head to the dressing room to quickly shower and change so I can get back to Toni.

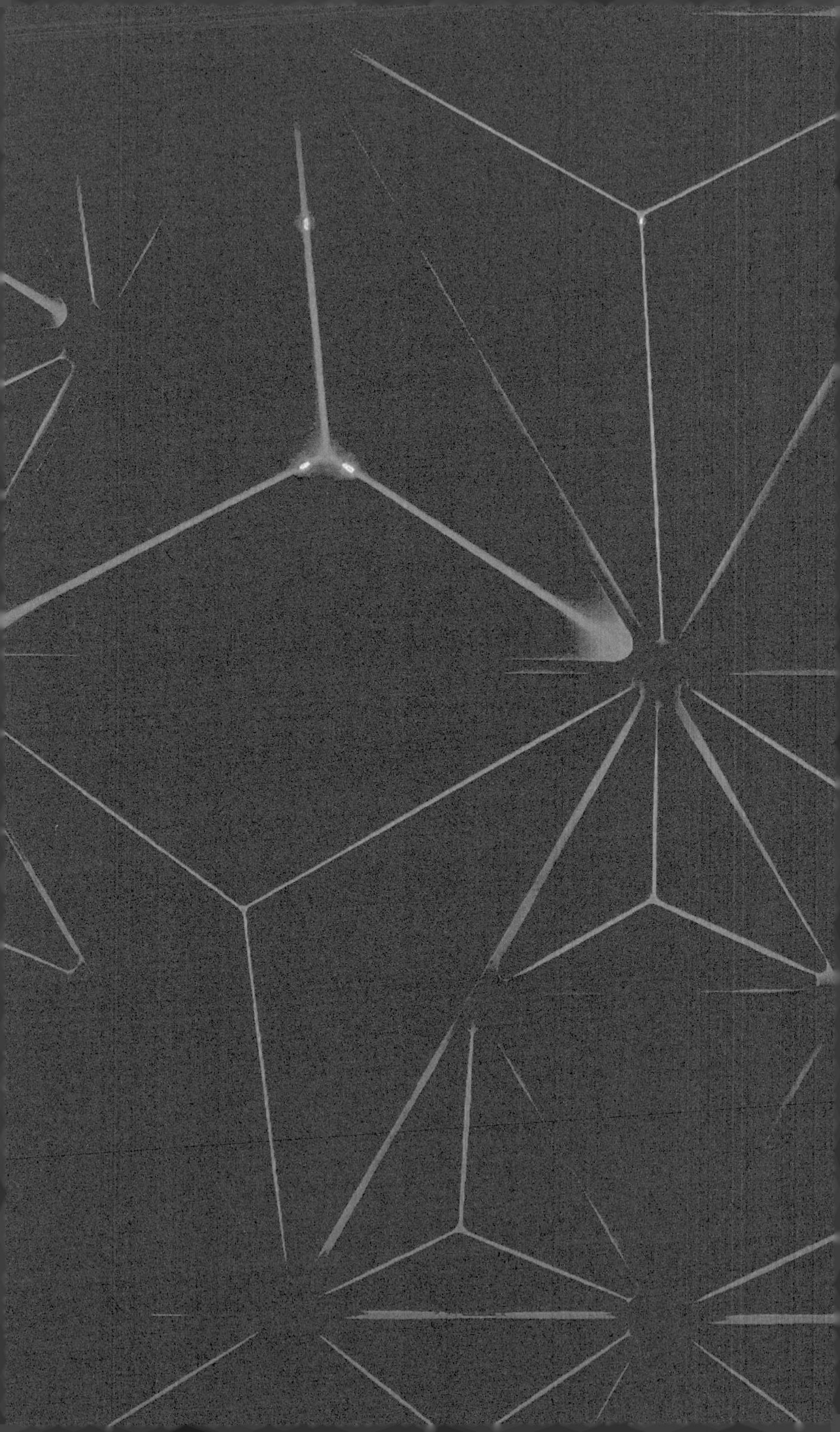

Chapter Thirty-Two
TONI

Iwake to the door closing. Shooting up, I see Luc standing near the door. Climbing from the bed, I rush to him, throwing my arms around him. I see him wince a little as I collide with his body. As I stare at his face, I can see the beginnings of a black eye.

"What happened?" I ask.

"Don't worry about it," he says, pulling me closer.

"Are you ok?"

"Al looks worse than I do. He got a couple of good hits in, but I got in more," he says, as he rests his cheek on the top of my head.

"I'm sorry you had to do this, Luc," I say, as I start to cry.

Tilting my face to his, he looks in my eyes and says, "Don't cry, baby. Yes, I'm still pissed at my brother for making a pass at my woman, but he's my brother and I will get over it in time. Believe me, once he knew that I knew what he did, he was remorseful."

Pulling away, I wipe my tears. "So, what are we going to do from here?"

"We're going to order something to eat and then we are going to make love until we both fall into an exhausted sleep," he says with a wolfish grin. "It could be all night."

I barely remember eating; I was too excited about the promise Lucius made me of a night's worth of making love. I know normally after a show he's exhausted, but I'm sure knowing he has a few days off gives him motivation to last all night.

And he does.

Light is just leaking into the room through the curtains when I finally drift off to sleep in Lucius's arms. I'm deliciously tender and know that any soreness I have when we wake later will be worth it. Lucius made sure I know without a doubt that he wants me regardless of what happened with his brother and Jas.

When I wake, I find myself alone in bed. I didn't hear him moving around in the bathroom but got up to check anyway. He wasn't in the room, but I find the note on the bed that I missed when I woke.

"Baby,

I had to go out for a bit. Meeting with the guys to sort shit out. Text me when you wake, and if we're done, I'll be back.

Love, L"

I get up and take a shower, figuring I'll give him time to make sure they sort things out. I'm only scared that it will mean I'll have to go home, but I will if I have to. I'm still tempted to go anyway. If I could have gotten a flight out yesterday when I was pissed, I would be on my way home right now. But by the time I looked, I'd missed the last flight out.

Once I'm finished with the shower, I quickly pull on sweats and a tank top. Searching for my phone, I find it in my bag where I dumped it on the floor yesterday when I stormed into the room. I pull it out to find it dead. I root around looking for my charger and plug it in. Sitting at the desk, I turn my notebook on and log into Facebook.

Worst mistake I've made. I look on the group page and find a video someone took of Luc and Al fighting. I want to stop looking, but I can't. The two of them are in a rage and full out brawling. I see the guys trying to break them up and Jas taking a swing at Al. I hold my hand to my mouth to cover my horror at seeing the video. My next worst mistake is to read the comments; tons of people are going to be banned.

I notice that Jas is on in Messenger. I pop open a message window and type a message to him.

Me: *Jas, have you seen the video that was posted?*

It's not long before I see three dots indicating he's replying.

Jas: *What video?*

Me: *Go check. Looks like you and I may be busy for awhile.*

Jas: *Fuck, we don't need this shit.*

Me: *No kidding. This makes my decision a whole lot easier. Looks like this is only a quick trip for me rather than the extended stay I'd hoped for.*

Jas: *What the fuck are you talking about?*

Me: *I'm pretty sure it's going to be uncomfortable between Luc and Al and adding me to the mix will make it even worse. And I'm pretty sure the fans probably hate me now that they're assuming that y'all are breaking up cuz of this.*

Jas: *Sweetheart, you leave and it's gonna just prove them right that you're coming between them, which we all know is Al's fault. The fans will latch on to anything to try to get rumours started. They'll try to blame you regardless. People believe shit that isn't true all the time. You staying means that this can be put behind us, and it will be. Nic and Chris are with them right now knocking sense into them. I heard the ping and stepped away."*

Me: *FML, why does this have to happen to me? First the kiss picture and now this video! What's next, a sex tape?*

Jas: *I'd buy that!*

Me: *Not helping, Jas.*

Jas: *Sorry, sweetheart. Let's get started on this shit. I'll post a comment and turn off the commenting and then we can start sorting and removing people.*

"A pinned post on our page has stated that

anyone caught being abusive or bullying will be blocked from all social media for the band. While things have been quiet since the picture that caused this new rule, the recent video post has now stirred things up again. Lucius and Alucard are brothers and, on occasion, do get into fights, just as Christoph, Nicholai, and I do on occasion. We are guys and sometimes we get into physical altercations, but at the end of the day, we are brothers and we will forgive one another. Lucius and Alucard will forgive one another, and Toni is an innocent party in this and should not be abused or bullied for the action Alucard instigated. The band is not breaking up and Lucius is still off the market. ~J"

I open a tab in my browser with all the social media accounts.

Me: I'll start with the earliest comments while you start with the latest and we'll work toward the middle?

Jas: *Sure. Btw I told Luc you're up and busy working like I will be.*

Me: *He pissed?*

Jas: *Not at you. Mostly at the person who posted*

the video, since he hoped to make sure that the coast was clear before he laid into his brother. The last thing he wanted was to be caught fighting with his brother, knowing rumours would start. If it makes you feel any better, Al is really sorry. He knows how badly he fucked up.

It didn't really make me feel any better. I just knew my relationship with Al would never be the same. Unlike how the guys can fight and be over it, I'm not made like that. I sigh and get started on ejecting people from the group, more people are added to the master list we'd made the first time people were removed.

I'm so lost in working that I don't even hear Luc return to the room. I only notice him when he starts to rub my stiff shoulders. Dragging my attention from my screen, I look up at him. He smiles down at me before leaning in and kissing me. I kiss him back, not caring if I end up ignoring helping Jasper in order to allow this divine man to take me to bed. Him kissing me can make me forget everything.

When he pulls away, I can't help but whimper at the loss. The gleam in his eyes makes me shiver. He knows he has me. He grabs my hand

and pulls me up into his arms and angles my head to kiss me deeper than before. I can feel his desire for me; his body has the same response as mine does, and I know I'm wet for him.

Wrapping my arms around his neck, I groan when I can't pull his hair like I used to. I hate that he cut it. I wrap one of my legs around his, trying to demand that he lift me. He does and I wrap my legs around his hips, slowly grinding myself into him. If my eyes were open I know I'd see dark blue irises filled with lust looking back at me.

My back hits the bed and I refuse to loosen my hold, for now happy just to be kissing. I moan as he rocks his hips, grinding against me, one of his hands sliding under my tank top. I shiver as he gently rolls a nipple between his fingers. I buck against him, completely turned on. He leans back to pull off his shirt and mine. He shimmies my pants and soaked underwear down my legs, and I kick them off while he makes quick work of his pants.

Back between my legs, I feel his tip pushing against my wet entrance, his breath panting against my neck. "What do you do to me?" he asks.

"The same thing you do to me," I reply in a throaty, breathless voice.

He sinks into my waiting heat, pausing when he's as deep as he can be. "Marry me, baby," he demands.

"Yes," I scream, as he begins to move his hips. Lifting mine, I match his pace. Sure, it may be too soon for marriage, but I know I don't want anyone else; his brother kissing me proves that. If anything came out of that debacle, it's that not any hot man could take his place. Not that I want anyone to take his place.

Just because I agreed, it doesn't mean I want to rush into getting married. There's still so much we need to know about one another, but that will come in time. I do know that I'm not going to let him get out of getting me a pretty ring, one that I would be proud to wear. But I'll have to tackle that later when I am not lost in my desire for this man. The man who owns me heart, body, and soul.

About
THE AUTHOR

A. Kelly Sweeney grew up as a hopeless romantic, devouring romance books like they were going out of style. The thrill of chasing words for the HEA is still something she loves to do, either through reading or her own dabbling with writing.

When not writing or reading, she can be found spending time with her family. She loves watching her two children discover the world around them. Although she and her husband are polar opposites, she loves the fact that they can find common ground with their love of movies and music. Date nights include checking out new releases or hitting up concerts in the city.

To keep up to date head over to her Facebook page
www.facebook.com/AKellySweeneyAuthor/
or her reader group Sweeney's Twisted Entourage

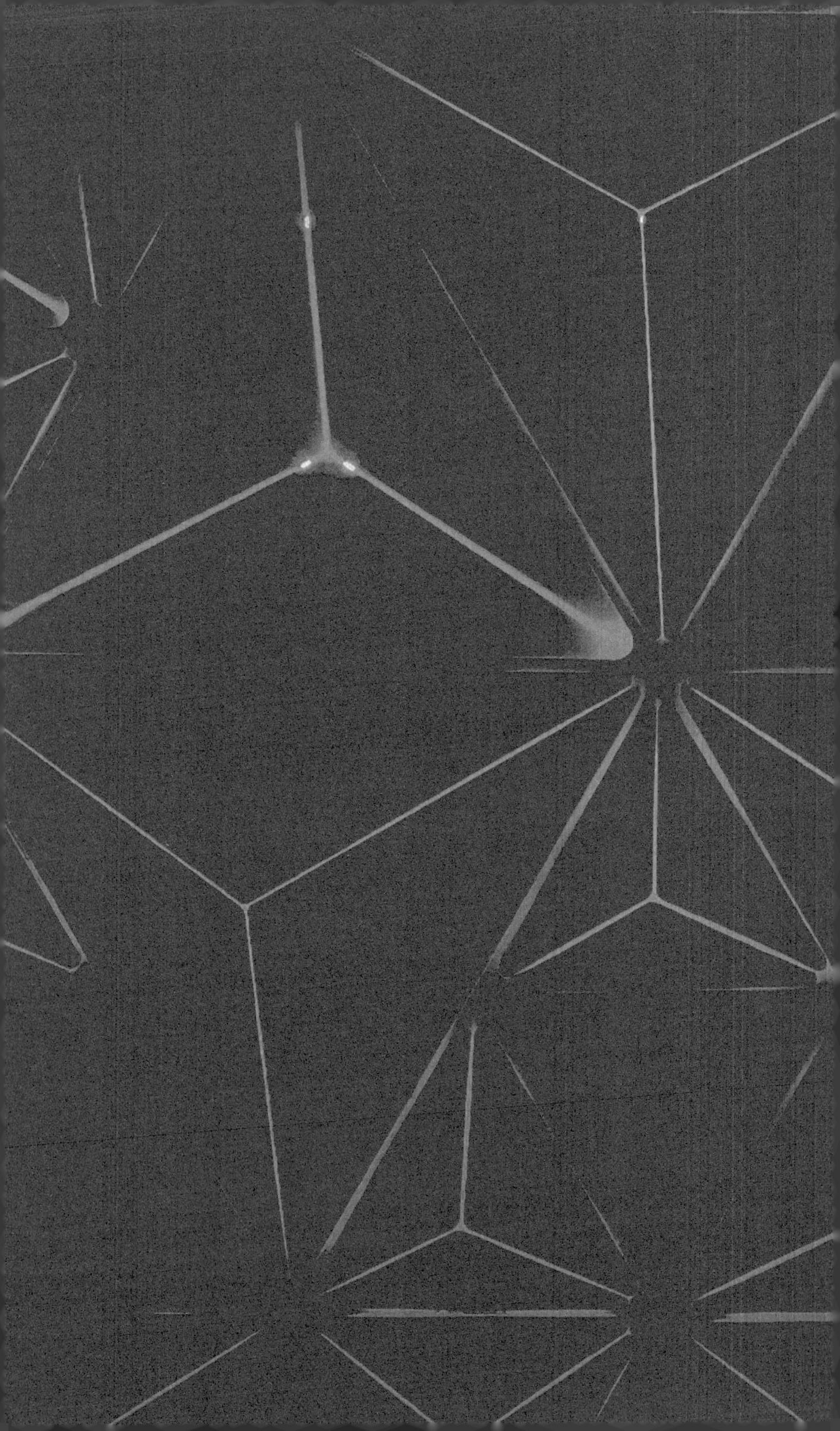

Acknowledgments

First, I need to thank Cora Kenborn and Derek Adam for getting me to get out of my own way. Both of you encouraged me to follow my dreams, and without that, I wouldn't have taken the leap of faith to have done this. Fear was holding me back, and both of you helped me to realize that not everyone will like what I write, but those who do, I hope to touch or inspire. From the bottom of my heart, I thank you for the encouragement that you've given me.

There's a ton more authors I'd love to thank who've been there with advice and offers of help along my journey to make this happen. If it hadn't been for your wisdom and helpfulness, I'd never have gotten through everything I needed to in order to hit the publish button.

There aren't enough words in the world that can give my thanks for the help you've given me. Jacob Chance and Marley Valentine, the two of you have been my biggest sources of information, and I'm so glad that you have helped not only me, but others looking to pursue the path of publishing. Without you, I'd be feeling even more overwhelmed about the whole process.

I need to thank my cover designer Raven Designs for bringing an idea I had to life. Thanks for being patient with me as I figured out what I wanted, and then making it happen. I'm looking forward to working together on our next project.

Thank you to Raven Designs for using your formatting skills and making everything look amazing between the covers. Without you, this book wouldn't look as great as it does when reading.

Shauna, where do I begin? As nervous as I was to share my work with you, knowing that you would be keeping a critical eye out for errors, I'm so glad I took the chance to let you read and edit for me. It was fun watching you work your magic with helping to improve what I already had. Somewhere along the way the nervousness changed to excitement, and anxiousness settled to know your overall thoughts. We took a chance on each other, both wanting to break into the business, and now our names are in print for the world to see. I hope that this gets your name coming up as someone to consider next time they need editing done.

Next, thank you, Arien, for always being there. You've helped me with finding my visual inspiration for a few of these guys, and I'm sure it was no small feat, but fun to ogle over men. You were quick to jump in and help me with plot holes you found while beta reading and pushing me to keep going so you had more. Your suggestion to run with a wishful thought made me realize something was missing, and a little drama doesn't hurt.

Misty, you've been amazing to help with plot holes and bouncing ideas off you. Plus the minor suggestions during beta reading helped. Thank you for all your help and encouragement, especially when I was ready to throw in the towel and keep this story as just for fun. You've helped to push me to keep toward making this dream come true. I cannot thank you enough for helping to ease my stress when I've needed it! And of course, thanks for sending pics of hotties to make me smile and inspire me with.

My other small band of betas; Denise Long, Cheril Olmsted, Meghann Martin, Jamie Lombard, Sarah Delong and Diane Hamilton. Thank you for your feedback and taking a chance on reading my work to help me figure out where I needed to work on things. Without you, I can't begin to improve my writing to know what needs to be fixed. I look forward to our next adventure when the next book is ready for your eyes.

My family. Thank you for all your love and support with wanting to make this a reality. You never stopped cheering me on and pushing me. Andrew, jokingly you've pushed me to exceed goals I made while writing. You pushed me to surpass my goal of a daily word count several times and cheered with me when I hit the joke of 10k not once but twice. My kids, you never know how much I love you and how you are part of the driving force for me to make this dream a reality. I'm showing you that you can make your dreams come true, even if you don't have faith in yourself to do so. You never complained about my endless hours of sitting at my computer writing, ignoring you with having my headset on listening to my playlist as I typed away because I knew daddy was there for your needs.

And lastly you, the readers and bloggers. Thank you for taking a chance on an unknown author like me. I hope you've enjoyed this story and will enjoy the rest of the guys from Twisted Tragic. Their stories will be coming, I promise. Without you taking the chance on reading me, I wouldn't have the opportunity to be sharing my work with anyone. Everyone has a story, and I know I have more running around in my head that I would love to share with you. So, thank you from the bottom of my heart for giving me a shot. I look forward to hearing what your thoughts are.